KING OF THE WILDS

ROSETHORN VALLEY FAE #3

TASHA BLACK

13TH STORY PRESS

13th Story Press

PO Box 506

Swarthmore, PA 19081

13thStoryPress@gmail.com

TASHA BLACK STARTER LIBRARY

Packed with steamy shifters, mischievous magic, billionaire superheroes, and plenty of HEAT, the Tasha Black Starter Library is the perfect way to dive into Tasha's unique brand of Romance with Bite!

Get your FREE books now at tashablack.com!

KING OF THE WILDS

1

MIRANDA

Miranda Cannon stepped gingerly between the trees, trying her best not to snag her clothes or lose a shoe. Her boss demanded that she look "office ready" at all times, which in his mind meant two-inch heels and a tailored suit.

But today, Miranda's office was a mosquito-ridden cove in the woods on the border between Rosethorn Valley and Tarker's Hollow. And she was pretty sure the mud from the recent storms was trying to eat her Jimmy Choos right off her feet.

And it was all just because some worker bee stopped paying attention and took a nasty tumble.

"It was right here," Larry, the foreman of the current job, turned to tell her, eyes round as saucers. "This is where Joey saw the lights."

Miranda looked around.

She wasn't exactly the outdoorsy type, but she couldn't detect anything unusual about this part of the forest. It was the same goopy, muddy path that they had used to get here - between thickets of bushes and stands of giant trees.

All around them, birds and other noisy creatures were yelling at each other and the air was humid enough to make her hair try to escape its bun and hightail it back to the city.

"So one of your men allegedly saw some lights here," she confirmed. "What kind of lights, exactly?"

She'd investigated workplace injury claims before, and knew better than to come right out and admit anything had happened the way it was reported - at least not until she had all the facts.

"He said they were small and twinkling, with an... other-worldly glow," Larry replied in a low, careful voice, as if he thought the lights were going to appear right now and carry him off to Neverland.

"It's June, and this is suburban Pennsylvania," Miranda said, trying to hide her smile.

"And?" Larry asked.

"Don't make me spell it out for you," she pleaded.

But he didn't answer.

"Is it possible that the lights he saw were merely fire-flies?" she asked.

"Joey's a Jersey guy. He knows what fireflies are," Larry said, scowling at her. "This ain't them."

Miranda sighed.

"So he allegedly saw these little twinkling, glowing lights, and then what?" she asked.

"He followed them," Larry replied.

"Off the path?" Miranda asked in horror. She could not imagine lights pretty enough to lure her into the tangle of trees to ruin the rest of her clothes and get eaten alive by mosquitos.

"Yes," Larry said. "Follow me."

"Is that really necessary?" Miranda asked. "If this is some elaborate hoax to trick my employer into giving you guys overtime, there's no point bothering. It isn't going to happen. He'd sooner fire all of you and hire a completely new crew."

Larry drew himself up with an expression of injured pride.

"The Dolor corporation has flown my crew all over the country to break ground for his projects. If we wanted more money, we would ask. This is something else. Something... different."

"Lead the way," Miranda said, surrendering.

Larry held back the branches of some thorny-looking shrubbery to let her proceed deeper into the woods.

He stepped in behind her and let the branches snap back into place. It was darker off the path, where the trees met overhead without interruption.

Miranda had never been easily spooked, but something about the forest set her on edge. An inexplicable shiver of dread traced its icy fingers down her spine in spite of herself.

"This way," Larry said quietly.

She followed him through the trees. Everything was so green and lush. There was no sign that any other human had been here before, and she had to remind herself that if she had to, she could walk her way back out of it and reach town in a couple of hours, even without her car, which waited back at the dirt lot the workers used.

"Okay, this is where he fell," Larry said at length, pointing to a ravine just below them.

"Wow," Miranda murmured.

The ravine was steep with jagged rocks at the bottom. It was no wonder the man had been badly injured. He was probably lucky to have survived.

"After that, things got bad," Larry said solemnly.

"*After* that?" Miranda echoed.

"I know it sounds crazy, but he saw something in the woods," Larry said. "Something big and furry."

"A bear?" Miranda suggested. "Bear sightings are not unheard of around here."

"It was carrying a club," Larry said, shaking his head. "Joey said it smelled like sulfur. And when it got closer, he saw that it only had one big eye at the center of its face."

"Didn't he hit his head?" Miranda asked doubtfully.

"That wouldn't impact his sense of smell," Larry replied.

Miranda made a mental note to look into that.

"So what did this one-eyed bear do?" she asked.

"It wasn't a bear," Larry insisted. "It rushed through the trees at him. He could hear the branches thrashing around and then it made this loud snorting roar."

"Then what?" Miranda asked.

"Then Joey said he heard someone singing in the distance," Larry said.

"And?" Miranda asked, finding herself sort of intrigued in spite of herself.

"And it ran away," he said.

"I see," Miranda said. "Well, thank you for walking me through it. I'll be sure to pass along this information to our legal team."

"You don't believe me, do you?" Larry asked.

She didn't.

"It doesn't matter what I believe," Miranda said. "It's my job to ask the questions tand convey the information. Shall we head back?"

Larry nodded sullenly.

Well, she couldn't really blame the man. Miranda was feeling a bit sullen herself. She'd been hired as a high-level executive assistant, not a camp counselor. And while she was out wandering around the woods listening to ghost stories, her phone had been buzzing up a storm in her pocket.

"Is there someplace around here that I can make a call?" she asked Larry.

Larry looked at her like she had two heads and spread his arms wide, as if the forest were her personal phone booth.

"Someplace *indoors*," she said.

"There's an old cabin where we eat lunch if it rains," he said dubiously.

"Perfect," Miranda replied.

They marched on in silence until they got back to the trail.

Miranda was exhausted, and a nasty blister was developing on her right heel. It would be good to take a little break, catch up on calls and emails and then head up the path to her car.

At least she didn't have to report back to Mr. Ward until morning. Lately, her demanding boss was spending more time away from the office, doing God only knew what.

One path wound into another and at last Larry pointed to something in the woods.

"There ya go."

Miranda turned to behold a structure that could only be called a cabin by the most generous definition of the word. The corrugated metal roof was rusty and the little building itself was shedding blackened cedar shakes like a nervous cat.

"That's it?" she asked.

"That's it," he told her. "Make yourself at home."

"Only if I'm a cobweb," she muttered to herself.

"Pardon?" Larry asked.

"Nothing, uh, thank you," she said.

"No problem," he told her. "See ya."

Larry marched off while Miranda headed inside and lost herself in her business so quickly that she didn't have time to mind the dingy interior.

A few hours later, she was still spread out at the rickety table in the so-called cabin. She was almost halfway through the emails on her tablet, and the phone was still buzzing like an angry hornet.

Cullen Ward was a powerful man, with powerful contacts who weren't used to being patient. As his assistant, it was her job to stroke egos and smooth feathers without committing Mr. Ward to anything he didn't want to do.

The door to the cabin creaked open and a couple of guys came in to collect their things.

"Uh, Miss Cannon, we're heading out," one of them said. "Larry said we should walk you to your car."

She glanced back at her tablet. Three more emails had just popped up. If she could just get to the bottom of her inbox before the end of business hours, it would be much better than letting any of Mr. Ward's contacts wait for her to get home.

"I'll be okay on my own," she told him. "I just need a few more minutes."

"Suit yourself," he shrugged. "You know your way out?"

"Of course," she said. "I'll just follow the path"

He gave her a little wave and the men filed out.

She turned back to her email as the phone rang again.

The calls went on for a bit, but finally slowed enough for her to respond to a handful of email messages.

The next time she picked up the phone she had barely said hello when the call cut off.

She held it away from her ear and studied the black screen. Her phone was totally dead.

"Shoot," she said. Of course her charger was in her car.

She gave one last glance to her stuffed inbox on her tablet, and decided reluctantly that she'd better pack it in.

She stood up and stretched and then did a double take.

It was completely dark outside.

She must have lost track of time while she was wheeling and dealing in this stupid cabin. It wasn't the first time she had done something like this, and it wouldn't be the last. When Miranda really got in the groove, she tended to completely zone out.

She folded up her tablet and tucked it into the pocket of her jacket.

When she turned off the single lightbulb that dangled over the table the cabin was plunged into total darkness.

A little shiver of fear ran down her spine and she shook her head at her own silliness.

"You're a capable woman, not a frightened construction worker," she scolded herself as she felt her way to the door and headed outside.

Once she was out, she was thankful that the moonlight illuminated her surroundings enough for her to see where she was going.

If she had thought the nighttime would be quieter in the forest than the day, she was dead wrong. It seemed to be even louder than before. The shadowy trees echoed with the cries of birds and cicada songs.

She headed across the mossy forest floor back to the muddy path that led up through the woods to the dirt lot across the site where she'd left her car.

The light from the nearly full moon overhead was

enough to let her see where she was going, but she still found herself wishing for the flashlight on her phone.

She honestly felt a real sense of separation anxiety over the lack of the device that sometimes felt like an extension of herself. Thankfully, she'd be back at her car soon. If she remembered correctly, it was no more than a twenty-minute walk back.

The blister on her right heel burned painfully with every step. She was half-tempted to take off her shoes. But she shuddered at the thought of all the nasty little creatures that might be scuttling around underfoot.

She walked on, hoping it would go numb soon.

Bats squeaked and flew overhead. Presumably, they were eating some of the plentiful mosquitoes. She'd doused herself liberally with a moisturizing lotion that claimed to act as an insect repellent. But she was beginning to doubt its claims as she slapped at yet another pesky bite. At this rate, she would be eaten alive soon, bats or no bats.

At least her path was starting to look familiar. That was good.

She squinted her eyes in the darkness. There was something in the trees, a small building, its roof glinting a little in the moonlight.

Funny, she didn't remember seeing any buildings on the way down here.

She took a few more steps toward it and almost began to cry.

It was the cabin again. She must have gone in a complete circle somehow.

She let out a long breath and felt sorry for herself for a count of ten.

Then she inhaled, ready to find her way home.

The path back to the car wasn't that complicated. She

had obviously just been lost in thought and made a wrong turn somewhere along the way. Or maybe it was that things looked a little different in the darkness.

But she wasn't helpless. She would find her way back.

This time, when she had gotten about five minutes away from the cabin, she saw a second path branching off from the first that she hadn't noticed before.

It was narrow, and she didn't really remember taking a narrow path to get here. But she had probably just been distracted with her phone buzzing every two seconds.

She headed into the trees on the tighter path. Assuming this was the right trail, she should be back at the car within fifteen minutes.

She was already picturing the frozen mac and cheese she planned to stick in the microwave when she got home, and the crisp, cold diet ginger ale with condensation running alluringly down the can.

A sudden burst of light in the darkness roused her from her fantasy.

She blinked and looked around, but it was already gone.

That was odd. Maybe she was just getting lightheaded. It had been a while since her last meal, and she didn't function well on low blood sugar.

She kept walking, picking up the pace a little. It would probably be best to get to the car as soon as possible. She needed to get home.

The night air was cooler but still heavy with moisture. A bead of sweat rolled down her spine.

A tiny light appeared before her again. This time, it glowed long enough that she was sure it was there.

Then another light appeared.

And another.

The first light winked out and more appeared, further down the path.

They were too big to be fireflies.

Miranda rubbed her eyes, wondering if she was losing her mind.

You haven't had anything to eat or drink since breakfast, she told herself. *And that idiot Larry told you about spooky lights in the woods and put the thought in your head.*

But when she took her hands from her eyes, the lights were still glowing in front of her, twinkling and moving, as if urging her forward.

They seemed to be moving right along with the path, though the path was almost impossible to make out now, since the glowing lights were brighter than the moonlight filtering through the trees.

She took a deep breath and continued, moving slowly to be sure of the ground beneath her feet.

You're being an idiot, Miranda, she told herself. *They're not evil lights leading you into a ravine. It's probably just big, healthy Pennsylvania lightning bugs.*

One buzzed past her face, and she swore she saw a tiny glowing human body with whisper-thin wings before it winked out and darted further down the path.

Now her imagination was really working overtime.

"One foot in front of the other," she whispered to herself.

The pain in her heel and the humidity faded away until there was only the pounding of her heart and the cold sweat prickling at her forehead.

Why did the pounding of her heart seem so loud?

She realized that the birds and cicadas had stopped their song.

An instant later she heard thrashing through the trees to her left side.

The twinkling lights seemed to shiver as a whole and then swarm around her, preventing her from being able to see a single step ahead on the narrow path.

"No," she murmured to herself.

But there was no place to hide. She was lit up like a Christmas tree by whatever these things were, blinded by their light so she couldn't escape.

The movement drew closer. She could hear the snapping of individual branches. Whatever it was, it was right on top of her.

The breeze carried its smell to her - a rotten, evil odor like a combination of spoiled meat and the tiger cages at the Philly Zoo.

Miranda closed her eyes and screamed.

There was an answering cry from somewhere in the woods to her right - low and throaty and raw.

Her own scream cut off instantly at the haunting sound of it.

Then the trees began to tremble and crash on the right side of the path as well.

She wrapped her arms around herself and sank to her knees.

Thunderous footsteps, almost like giant hoofbeats, rushed her. Something huge and hairy was coming at her from the left. And she saw a hint of sleek fur and the moonlit outline of antlers on the right.

Oh, God. There are two of them.

They were going to rip her to pieces in their turf war.

She was going to die here in the woods. And Larry would stand over her grave and say, "I told you so."

2

BRON

Bron stormed through the trees in the form of a giant stag.

There was a woman.

What was she doing out here?

Something about her primal scream left him undone, though the King of the Wilds was a fierce warrior and not one to be shaken by a mortal scream.

He smashed past saplings and leapt over fallen logs. Fingers of foliage reached out to caress him as he passed, but he had no time to commune with them.

He could see her now, huddled on the ground, arms over her head.

Mischievous will o' the wisps surrounded her like a cloud, their light showing the bloodthirsty fachan exactly where to find her.

The fachan itself was nearly there. Bron could smell its horrible carrion breath.

He let go of his stag form and shifted back into a man shape, then threw back his head and roared again, calling to his own to help him.

The woman trembled.

On the other side of her the fachan yelped in surprise as the roots of the nearest tree reached out to trip him.

The enormous monster hit the forest floor so hard Bron could feel the wet ground reverberate under his feet.

He roared a third time and was gratified to see the awful thing drag itself further into the forest, away from the woman.

Bron stood over her, feeling a surge of pride and possessiveness.

"Woman, are you hurt?" he asked.

She wasn't hurt, he already knew that. But he hoped it would make her feel better to answer the question.

"I'm f-fine," she murmured, slowly lowering her arms from over her head as the will o' the wisps dispersed.

She gazed up at him - her eyes were large, dark, and filled with fear. They were set off by the extreme paleness of her moonlit skin and the bright, fiery red of her hair.

"Come," he said, offering her his hands.

She took them and allowed him to help her to her feet.

He was surprised to see how tall she was. He still towered above her, but she was a very healthy specimen as mortals went.

He felt an odd pang of kinship towards this other large being with flame-colored hair like his own.

"What was that?" she asked him, looking over her left shoulder into the woods.

Who are you? would have been a more common question for a shivering mortal, but she seemed utterly unafraid of Bron's bare, muscled chest and impressive height.

"That was called a fachan," he told her. "It's a one-eyed, hairy harbinger of hell."

"What did it want?" she asked.

"To club you over the head and eat you… eventually," he replied. "They like to play with their food first."

"Thank you for saving me," she said earnestly.

He smiled at her in spite of himself.

Bron had always enjoyed mortals. He understood all living things to some extent, even the fachan, in its way. But Bron was considered too big-hearted by many of his fae brothers. He was vulnerable to small, fragile things.

Including humans, despite the risks.

Mortals like this woman were very reckless with their short lifespans. They had so little to lose, and it made them dangerous. Bron's nanny had warned him since he was a child to give mortals a wide berth.

But he was no child now.

And he'd never seen another mortal quite like this woman.

"Let's get you someplace safe," he said gruffly, trying not to let himself listen to her heartbeat.

She nodded and took a step, wincing when she did.

"You said you weren't hurt," he said accusingly.

"Well, I hurt my foot, but that was before all this," the woman replied. "I'm not used to the woods. And these shoes are the worst."

They looked together at her inadequate footwear. They really were terrible. Typical mortal female nonsense with pointed toes and spiky heels designed to give an illusion of tallness.

Many creatures tried to appear bigger to ward off predators. But this human was of ample height. She had no need for such things.

"Take them off," he said.

She removed them meekly.

"I will carry you," he told her.

Her eyes grew larger still, but she didn't protest. She merely extended her arms to hold onto him as he scooped her up.

She felt incredible, warm and soft, her curves conforming to his hard muscle.

"What were you doing out here?" he asked her, trying to keep his mind off the feel of her body against his.

"I work for the developer who's buying this land," she told him. "There was an accident the other day and he wanted someone on the ground to ask questions."

"Did he know you were going out alone after dark without proper footwear?" Bron demanded.

"Uh, the footwear is company policy," Miranda said. "But it's my fault it's so late. I didn't start off alone. I was working in the cabin and lost track of time. Everyone else went home."

"I see," Bron said.

He didn't see though. The woman should not have been left unattended. The woods were full of monsters. Not that the mortals knew this. They were often blind to anything their meager senses could not explain.

This particular mortal was taking the news strangely well.

"So were you telling me the truth about the fachan?" she asked.

"Yes," he said. "They're very dangerous."

"Then why haven't I heard of it before?" she asked.

"It's not commonly found here," he told her carefully.

"In Pennsylvania?" she asked.

He chuckled at that. "Sure."

"And what were those... lights?"

"How much do you know about faeries?" he asked.

She fell quiet.

"What about magic?" he asked.

Still no answer.

"Well, there's no point beating around the bush," he said. "What you saw were will o' the wisps. They're evil fae that lead mortals into danger."

"Why?" she asked.

He hadn't expected that question.

"I suppose they think it's funny," he told her.

"And you?" she asked.

Interesting.

He had thought that maybe she wouldn't sense his magic. After all, he looked like a human male, except for being much larger and clearly stronger than most human males.

But he was beginning to realize there was something about her too, something... other than mortal.

"I am the King of the Wilds," he told her proudly.

"Oh," she said. "It's nice to meet you, your majesty."

She couldn't bow since she was cradled in his arms, but he suspected she would have if she'd been on the ground. Instead, she lowered her eyes.

"You may call me Bron," he decided.

"I'm Miranda," she replied.

"Pleasure to make your acquaintance," he said.

"So why were you in the woods?" she asked him.

"Some of my kind broke through the veil between our worlds, and are causing chaos on your side," he told her. "My brothers woke me to help them recapture the monsters and put them back where they belong."

"You were asleep?" Miranda asked.

"For centuries," he explained. "One of my brothers gave these monsters succor. And all of us were punished."

"Well, I'm glad you're here now," Miranda said, resting her cheek against his chest.

Something about this simple, trusting gesture moved him.

He lowered his face to inhale her scent.

She was enchanting, her floral perfume mixing with the more interesting coppery scent of sweat.

He found himself longing to bed her.

It had been a few centuries, and he was clearly in need of a consort. But this human would hardly do. He needed a more sturdy partner for what he had in mind. Not some mortal that couldn't find her way out of a forest.

"So you and your brothers just come into the woods and look for monsters?" she asked after a moment.

"Yes," he told her. "And I'm going to take you to them so we can decide what to do with you until the fachan is captured."

"No, no," she said dismissively. "I have to get home. I've got work to do and I need a shower and something to eat."

"The fachan got close to you, too close," he told her. "He has tasted your scent. You are no longer safe."

She shivered in his arms and he cuddled her closer without thinking about it, brushing his lips across the top of her head.

"Oh, there's my car," she said happily.

He had brought her out to the lot where the workers had been parking.

A single carriage remained.

"I'll ride with you," he told her. "I can tell you where to go. I'm meeting them at a diner in the village of Tarker's Hollow. It's called the Barry White Diner. You can have food there and we can make a plan."

"I know the Barry White Diner," she told him. "I'm from

Tarker's Hollow. We used to go there all the time in high school."

"Excellent," he said. "It is decided then."

He was very sure she would accompany him. No one who had once eaten at the marvelous Barry White Diner would ever turn down a return visit.

"Fine," she said. "I'll go and meet your brothers. Pancakes actually sound really good right now. But I'm not agreeing to be under house arrest until you find the fachan. It's just a meal and a conversation."

"Of course," he told her. "As you wish."

He had to deposit her on the ground so that she could open the door to the carriage the humans simply called a car.

He was surprised to find how cold and empty his arms felt without her in them.

She dug for her keys and unlocked the car, hopping in the driver's side. Bron got in as well, and she drove them carefully down the long, rutted track that led back to Rosethorn Valley proper.

"They're not going to let you in without a shirt," she said, glancing over at him.

He noticed how her eyes lingered on the tattoos that decorated his pectoral muscles. She was correct. He'd borrowed a shirt from his brother when he'd last visited.

"I have one of my boss's shirts in the back," she said, indicating a plastic bag on the rear seat.

Bron grabbed it and opened it up. He highly doubted that her boss's shirt would fit someone of his size, but he was willing to humor her.

Miranda kept her eyes on the road while he slipped it on.

He was surprised to find that it did fit over his arms. It

was tight in the chest and biceps, but he was still able to close it.

"Will this be okay?" he asked.

"Perfect," she said, smiling at him.

He felt another wave of some deep emotion and turned to look out the window instead of considering its source.

Beware mortals. They have nothing to lose.

But the general advice felt hollow in the face of this warm and fascinating mortal he had just saved from certain death.

3

MIRANDA

Miranda stepped into the bright interior of the Barry White Diner and immediately was carried back in time to the sounds and smells of high school.

The orange Naugahyde booths were the same as always, as were the waitresses in their skirts and aprons. As a matter of fact, Miranda recognized a few faces. The staff here was loyal. They must be doing something right.

She could taste bacon, eggs, and happiness on the air. This diner was a refuge for anyone seeking company or a bite to eat when the rest of the world was sleeping. It was literally the only place open late in the tiny town.

Booths full of teens giggled and shared plates of French fries while the old-timers at the counter sipped coffee and traded gossip. At this time of night, the Barry White was mainly host to the youngest and oldest customers in Tarker's Hollow.

Someone waved from a big corner booth.

"Here we go," Bron said, placing a big hand at the small of her back to lead her toward the table.

Two enormous men, one light-haired, one dark, barely fit in the booth. They were accompanied by two women.

Two very familiar women.

Miranda froze in her tracks.

"What's wrong?" Bron asked.

"What is the meaning of this, brother?" the dark-haired one demanded.

The group of teens in the booth next to them giggled at the outburst.

"*This* is who you're working with?" Miranda asked Bron. "Is this some kind of joke?"

Bron looked back and forth between the group at the table and Miranda, a confused expression on his handsome face.

"Come sit down," the woman with the longer dark hair said quietly, patting the seat next to her. "Let's not make a scene. I'm Sara. This is Tabitha and the guys are Dorian and Tristan."

Miranda thought about it for a second.

Her stomach growled, making her mind up for her.

"Miranda," she said, sitting down.

"We know," said the woman with the shorter dark hair. "And I'm telling you right now, if you start playing that game with us, we will play back."

Shit.

"What game?" Bron asked, his brow furrowed.

In the light of the diner, Miranda could see Bron's masculine features better. His hair was almost the same bright copper as hers and fell around his shoulders in waves. His light beard was just a bit darker. But his eyes were his most striking feature. They were a deep green, like smoky emeralds, or a lush field after a rainstorm.

His gaze was so intense that she could barely meet it.

"She *compels* people," Tabitha said. "We watched her do it at the presentation about the development of the mansion property."

"Is this true?" Bron asked.

He looked fascinated, not angry.

"I-I'm not really sure," Miranda admitted. "I've always had a way with people, but it's gotten stronger recently."

"Why is she here?" Dorian asked.

"I was patrolling my woods and I heard something," Bron said. "The fachan was about to attack her."

Tristan hissed in a sympathetic breath.

"Why were you in the woods in the middle of the night?" Tabitha asked.

"One of the surveyor's guys got hurt," Miranda explained. "My boss wanted me to check it out. I got caught up in work stuff, and ended up heading out really late."

"Someone got hurt?" Sara asked.

Miranda nodded. "He's in intensive care right now."

"What happened to him?" Sara asked.

"I don't know," Miranda admitted. "At first I thought what the foreman said was all nonsense. But I guess the same thing happened to him that just happened to me."

"Lured by will o' the wisps," Bron explained, "then attacked by the fachan."

"Except the workman said he heard singing before the monster ran away," Miranda said.

"Hey, that was you," Tabitha said, elbowing Sara.

Sara grinned.

Miranda noticed they had matching tattoos on their left hands, inky black vines starting at their fingers and twining up around their wrists. The two men had them, too. It was as if they were in some kind of magical gang.

Miranda shook her head, willing herself to focus.

"Can someone please tell me what's going on?" she asked.

"Yes, but first we have to get food," Bron said. "What do you want?"

"The special - eggs, bacon, toast, coffee, everything," Miranda listed quickly. "Listen, can you order while I run and freshen up?"

Bron scowled at her.

"I'm not going to make a run for it in these shoes, if that's what you think," she said, barely resisting the urge to roll her eyes.

He scooted out of the booth and let her go.

She strode through the diner to the bathroom hallway in the back. Thankfully, she didn't know any of the teenagers or old folks here tonight.

After taking care of her needs, she washed her hands and face carefully.

It had been a very long day.

Work was stressful, as was her relationship with her boss. And lately, her own ability had been more strange and frightening than any of the rest of it.

But the face gazing back at her in the mirror looked more alive than it had in a long time.

Whatever was going on with her, the people out at that table seemed to know more about it than she did.

Of course, they saw her as an enemy to Rosethorn Valley since she worked for the man who was tearing down the historic mansion.

But they were working to rid the cliffside of the monsters that were loose there.

That was also in Cullen Ward's best interests.

If Miranda worked with them, she would really be helping her boss.

And maybe helping herself too, if they could help her understand her own ability to *compel* as Tabitha had put it.

There was a knock at the bathroom door.

"Come in," Miranda said. There were two stalls in the room, she wasn't entirely sure why anyone would knock.

"Hey," Sara said, slipping inside with her.

"Oh, hi," Miranda said.

"Listen, I know we all got off on the wrong foot," Sara said. "But I think we have a lot of priorities in common. And I think we can help each other with some of it."

"I was just thinking the same thing," Miranda admitted.

"Maybe it's a good idea to work together to capture the fachan," Sara said. "Your, um, ability complements our group's gifts. Just don't take it too badly if we try to convince you to see things our way when it comes to the mansion."

"I know I'm not going to change your mind," Miranda said. "And I won't try."

"Sounds like a deal to me," Sara said. "Friends for now?"

Miranda took the hand Sara offered and shook it. "Friends for now."

Sara smiled.

"Hey, what's with the tattoos?" Miranda asked, indicating Sara's left hand.

"Oh, wow," Sara said. "I guess that does seem weird. They're magical. They appeared on our hands when I became Dorian's queen. And the same thing happened for Tabitha and Tristan."

"You're...?" Miranda couldn't finish the sentence.

"A fairy queen?" Sara offered. "Yeah. How weird is that? Who knew my second grade Halloween costume could accurately predict my future? I guess I'm just lucky I didn't go as a zombie cheerleader that year."

A startled laugh came out of Miranda's lips.

Sara laughed too, and for a moment it felt like the beginning of a real friendship, not just a friendship *for now*. Miranda hadn't met many people who were willing to just open up to her the way Sara just did.

They left the bathroom together and headed back to the table, where two waitresses were already depositing an improbably large amount of breakfast foods.

"Wow," Miranda breathed.

"One thing to know when you hang out with these guys," Sara confided. "They eat *a lot*."

"My kind of people," Miranda said, smiling.

She glanced over at Bron and was happy to notice there were no tattoos on his left hand.

He raised his eyebrows as if asking why she was looking at him.

She gave him a quick smile and then focused on her meal, hoping he hadn't caught what she was looking for.

4
———

BRON

Bron stood on the soft carpet of Miranda's hotel room.

After a hearty meal, she had asked to come back here and change before heading into the woods to deal with the fachan.

Bron had insisted on accompanying her. The others would meet them at the parking area.

"Almost ready," Miranda called to him.

He hoped so.

Bron was most comfortable outdoors. Failing that, he preferred caves and cabins, and in a pinch, he was learning he could tolerate the basements and first floors of more modern structures.

In the fae realm, the jewel of his kingdom was his beautiful underground castle made up of round, cozy rooms with dim labyrinthine tunnels between them.

On the other hand, Miranda had described Tarker's Hollow's new Inn as bright and airy.

Bron appreciated the nature paintings in the lobby. But the fourth floor of a gigantic stone and mortar building, unsheltered by trees or mountains, was not a place where he liked spending time.

Miranda's presence made it more bearable though.

She had stoked his lust again a moment ago, wandering from the bathroom to the bedroom wearing nothing but a towel, water droplets sliding down her delicious flesh. Her hair had been down, the wet locks cascading down her back like liquid fire.

"You know we're just going back in the woods, right?" he'd barked out, turning away and trying to cover up the pang of passion he felt.

"I know," she'd said. "I just want to be clean, even for a few minutes."

He paced the soft carpet and peered out the giant windows into the darkness, hoping the fachan hated big buildings as much as he did.

She reentered, her hair pulled back in a tidy bun again, wearing bright pink breeches with a pink tunic on top and a pair of soft looking shoes without points on the heels.

"Sorry, my yoga stuff is all I have with me," she said. "Other than business suits, that is."

"This color is not good for sneaking," he said. "But you'll make good bait."

"Uh, thank you," she replied.

He drew in a breath.

"You don't like being thanked?" she asked.

"The folk do not like the burden it implies," he told her.

"Huh," she said. "I know someone else who says he hates thanks. I always thought it was because he was too rotten to say it himself."

Bron laughed.

He liked this woman. She said what she thought. This was a rare quality among his people.

She smiled back at him quizzically.

"Are you ready to go?"

"Of course," he told her.

They headed out of the room. The door clicked behind them and she checked to be sure it was locked.

"Elevator or stairs?" she asked when they reached the hall.

"Stairs, please," he said gratefully. She seemed to sense his discomfort in this place.

They headed down to the lobby, where a sleepy receptionist asked if they needed help.

"We're just heading out for a walk," Miranda replied.

The receptionist glanced at the clock on the wall, eyebrows high at the late hour, then shrugged and leaned back on her hand.

"I need to be a better liar," Miranda murmured when they reached the parking lot.

"My kind aren't good liars," Bron said.

"I've heard that before," Miranda said thoughtfully. "But lying is more than just saying something that isn't true. There are other ways to be less than honest."

"Yes," he agreed. "It seems you know more about my kind than I would have expected."

"Well, we've all read the fairytales," she said, unlocking the car.

They got in and buckled up. He watched as she started the car.

"You're from this town?" he asked.

She nodded.

"No wonder you're comfortable with magic," he said.

"What do you mean?"

"There's something about this place," he said. "You can just *feel* it. My brothers told me there was some kind of portal opened nearby that let the old magic back into this part of the world. I don't know if that's true, but there is definitely something special about this place."

She glanced at him. "I've always felt that way. But I could never put my finger on it."

"My kind have only recently returned," he told her. "But there's more than fae magic here. Maybe we'll learn more of it while we're monster hunting."

"Maybe," she said, gazing at the road in front of her.

He wondered suddenly what drove her. She worked hard and she wore no man's ring.

"What do you wish for, Miranda Cannon?" he asked impulsively.

Her eyes widened. "What do you mean?"

He shrugged.

"Right now I wish we could catch the fachan, so he doesn't eat me," she said lightly.

That wasn't what he had meant. But he let it go.

They had an adventure ahead. It was time to focus.

The road through Tarker's Hollow was already leading them over the bridge and into Rosethorn Valley.

Mist hung over the creek tonight, lending the little borough an extra air of mystery.

Fear began to twist around his heart.

What if something happens to her tonight?

But Bron would not allow that.

He just wouldn't.

5
___

MIRANDA

Miranda parked the car and then smoothed her hair down as best she could.

She wasn't going to work, but she was basically going to fight a monster with a group of people who didn't really like her.

And she was wearing a silly pink yoga outfit.

And, apparently, curls were going to escape from her bun, no matter how ruthlessly she crammed them back in.

"It looks nice," Bron said quietly.

She glanced over at him, feeling a little sheepish. "I just want it out of my way," she fibbed.

He nodded and gave her a half smile that made her insides do a little flop.

What is going on with me?

Miranda was usually the practical type. The fact that she was even standing here, after all she'd been through tonight, was out of character for her. And her inability to keep her thoughts, and her eyes, off of some random man she'd just met in the woods was causing her to question her very sanity.

Maybe she'd fallen in the woods earlier, and this was all some concussion-induced dream.

It sure didn't feel like one.

She pushed the thoughts aside as they got out of the car and headed to where the others were grouped around a flashlight.

Except that as she got closer, Miranda saw it wasn't a flashlight at all.

The blond one, Tristan, held a ball of glowing golden energy between his palms.

"Whoa," she breathed before she could stop herself.

"In our realm, Tristan is the King of Light," Bron told her. "And Dorian is the King of Darkness."

Holy crap. These guys really weren't kidding around.

"And what are you?" Miranda asked, trying to play it cool. "The king of mid-afternoon snacktime?"

Bron threw his head back and laughed. It was a deep, booming sound that made Miranda feel instantly at home.

"I'm the King of the Wilds," he told her. "The creatures and plant life are my domain."

She nodded. Somehow, that made perfect sense.

"Sara is a bard," Tabitha said. "She can sing magic songs. And I'm a mender. I fix broken things."

"Seriously?" Miranda asked.

She had never met anyone with powers like hers. Or anyone who was so direct about something so unusual. As much as these two had resented her ability to compel, it sounded like they had their own unfair advantages.

Maybe that was why she felt a sort of kinship with them, despite their differences. It was too bad the other women didn't feel the same.

"How does your magic work?" Sara asked Miranda. "Maybe we can use it against the fachan."

Miranda shook her head. "I don't really know," she admitted. "I never really thought about it as magic. It was just... something I could do. I've spent most of my life trying to restrain it. I've only recently tried to use it. I think it's getting stronger."

The other two women nodded.

"It's been like that with us for a while as well," Sara confided. "But it's definitely gotten more intense since these guys arrived on the scene."

"I guess that makes sense," Miranda said, unsure of whether it actually did or not.

"Let's find this thing," Bron said suddenly, surveying the tree line in a decidedly suspicious way.

"What's the plan?" Sara asked.

"Let's split up into groups of two," Tabitha suggested. "We can cover more ground that way. Just yell if you see anything. Tristan and I will go through the woods to the north of the trail. You and Dorian go south."

"We'll go straight down the path," Bron said to Miranda.

Miranda nodded, trying not to take it personally.

It was painfully clear that Tabitha wanted to split up because she didn't want to spend another minute with Miranda.

It doesn't matter if she likes me, Miranda told herself. *It's not like we're all going to be best friends or something. I'm just helping them with this one task.*

"Ready?" Bron asked.

His green eyes glimmered in the moonlight. He was the size of a mountain, but his expression was that of a kid on Christmas.

"You really love it out here, don't you?" she asked him.

"Oh yes," he replied. "Don't you?"

"I'm really more the indoors-y type," she admitted.

"You must not be doing it right," he told her as they started down the path.

"How am I doing it wrong?" she asked, laughing.

"First of all, those clothes you had on earlier were all wrong," he told her. "You can't enjoy the forest when you're fighting against it just to walk."

"That's fair," she said. "But I'm dressed pretty appropriately now. Why am I not loving it?"

"Because you're not paying attention," he said. "Listen."

She listened.

Night birds cried out and the cicadas made up a chorus behind the birdsong. Otherwise, it was silent except for the sound of their feet on the path.

"It's quiet, but kind of spooky," she offered.

"Why is it *spooky*?" he asked.

"The way the birds are crying out," she said. "It sounds like they're warning us off."

He chuckled. "That's a robin," he said. "Do you know why he's singing?"

"No idea," she admitted.

He listened for a moment.

"He's looking for a mate," he told her gruffly.

Something about this made her smile.

"I didn't think robins were nocturnal," she said.

"They aren't," he replied sadly. "There's too much light near your mortal cities. It's thrown him off."

"I guess he's not going to find a date after all," Miranda said.

"Not until morning, most likely," Bron told her.

"Well, I hope he finds her then," Miranda said.

Suddenly the birdsong wasn't so creepy.

"Just a moment," Bron said.

She paused.

He lifted his chin and let out an ethereal whistle in the same key the robin had been singing.

There was a moment of silence and then another bird-call from the trees.

A slight breeze and a rustle of feathers later and the King of the Wilds had a bird on his shoulder.

"It is night time, little friend," Bron told the creature softly.

The bird cocked his head.

"Rest now, find your mate in the morning," Bron said.

The robin chirruped out a low note and fluttered into a nearby tree.

"Now he's got it," Bron said with a smile. "Let's go."

Miranda couldn't reply or even move. She was frozen in amazement. This guy was like something out of Disney movie.

"This is my kingdom," Bron said simply, as if that explained everything.

He lifted his hands, palms up, to indicate the forest around them.

"Such as it is in this realm," he added with a touch of sadness.

"We haven't been kind to the environment," Miranda said quietly.

"There is still time to learn," Bron said as they walked on.

That smarted.

She knew acutely that he wasn't just talking about humans in general. Her own boss was at the forefront of tearing down trees and replacing them with concrete. It was as if he had a vendetta against nature.

She had sworn not to try to change the minds of this unlikely crew of monster hunters.

But they had made no such promises about changing hers.

"One of the realities of modern life is that individuals have fewer rights than corporations," she said.

It was an oft-repeated statement, but a true one, and hardly her fault.

"I have no idea what that means," Bron said.

"It means that big corporations, maybe you'd call them merchants, have more rights than people," she told him. "We can't always stop them from doing what they want."

"We are each responsible for our own actions," he said coldly. "And if any entity threatens our home and the ones we love, we should burn it to the ground."

He meant it. She could see the fierce scowl under his flame colored beard.

"Your realm sounds like an intense place," she said.

"All realms are worthy of intense protection," he said. "Your kind will learn, or they will pay with their very existence."

She buttoned her lip and walked on.

She shouldn't keep finding herself accidentally invested in this relationship. It was bound to be a short one.

And it was embarrassing that her foolish heart couldn't tell the difference between physical appreciation for hot, wild-looking man and caring about his opinion of her.

Bron walked on beside her, seemingly unaffected by any worries of his own.

A moment later, a feeling of wrongness overcame her. She couldn't explain it, but it chilled her to her bones.

"Bron," she murmured.

"I know," he replied.

The cicadas had gone quiet. The only sound in the night air now was the sound of their footsteps.

No.

There were more footsteps than that. Something was thrashing toward them from just off the path.

Terror made her heart threaten to stop beating.

"*Brothers,*" Bron roared.

The sound echoed off the trees and she heard footsteps coming from all around now.

They were coming. The others would help her. She didn't know why the thought comforted her - she barely knew them.

She unfroze and tried to spot the thing coming for her in the trees. It was closer now. She could see the foliage waving wildly.

This part of the path followed a steep hillside. It would be hard to run.

"Stay behind me," Bron growled.

She obeyed reluctantly.

If this thing was her destiny, she wanted to face it.

Dorian and Sara joined them first, from behind.

She spun to see Dorian drawing his forearms together and bowing his head as Sara held out a huge shard of glass.

Inky darkness seemed to issue from Dorian's chest, tendrils of it reaching into the forest as if searching for the fachan.

Soft light came from the opposite direction, finally showing her the outline of the creature as she peeked around Bron's big body.

It was larger than she remembered, larger than life. And it lumbered toward her with a singular focus.

Tristan sprinted toward her from behind the thing. He ran around it, allowing it a wide berth.

As he drew closer, she felt her fear retreat and warmth fill her chest once again, like morning sunshine.

He's the King of Light...

Tabitha followed close behind him as if the two were one.

The beast howled, as if sensing that it was outnumbered.

But its appetite for Miranda seemed only to grow, and it lumbered closer still.

She could smell its rotten stench now. It was almost close enough to touch, its movements gone frantic in its hunger.

"*Easy, fachan,*" Bron intoned. "We don't want to fight you."

Miranda watched as its movements gentled.

But it was still moving toward her.

Sara began to sing, holding out the mirror shard in front of her as she did.

The mirror brought you to this place,
  Broken mountain lacking grace,
  Thinning forest, slender trees,
  Poison in the noxious breeze,

THE THING SWUNG around toward Sara menacingly, as if it knew shew was trying to trick it.

She slipped a little on the muddy ground, but managed to catch herself and keep singing.

Seeking the woman for a meal,
  Though truly in your bones you feel,
  She is made of city light,
  Too easy to catch, too weak for a fight,

. . .

HE LUNGED FOR SARA AGAIN.

This time she lost her footing and stopped singing.

Dorian was buried in the darkness he was bringing forth, so he didn't see what was happening. And the others were too far away to grab her.

Miranda acted on instinct.

"*STOP*," she cried, and power seemed to spill out of her like an invisible wave.

The whole world around them seemed to pause for an instant.

The big beast stopped mid-lunge as if gravity itself had commanded it.

Sara stopped falling.

In the heartbeat that followed she found her footing and hurriedly continued her song.

BACK TO YOUR *home you choose to go,*
Where mountain caps are peaked in snow,
Where worthy prey is swiftly found,
And mortals to the land are bound.

THE BIG BEAST bowed his head.

Dorian's obsidian shadows fluttered in and closed around it.

Before Miranda's eyes, she saw it melt down into smoke and disappear in to the shard of mirror in Sara's trembling hands.

The forest was silent for a moment, except for their ragged breathing.

"What was that?" Tabitha asked Miranda after a moment.

She wasn't talking about the creature. She was talking about whatever Miranda had done.

"I-I don't know," Miranda admitted.

Tabitha studied her suspiciously.

"She saved my life," Sara said to Tabitha. "You saved my life. Thank you."

"You're welcome," Miranda told her. "I've never done anything quite like that before."

Dorian put an arm around Sara and smiled at Miranda. "I'm glad you did it when you did."

"Does no one care how dangerous that kind of power is?" Tabitha asked.

"I would never do that if someone weren't in danger," Miranda said quickly. "I'm honestly not sure if I could do it again anyway. I don't even know how I did it this time."

"We're all tired," Bron said firmly. "Time for bed."

"No one wants to talk about this?" Tabitha pleaded. "That was like something one of these monsters would do."

Miranda felt tears sting her eyes.

Don't give them the satisfaction.

"Is that really what you think I am?" she asked, letting her temper get the better of her. "So I'm just another creature to you, something for you to fear, something for you to hunt?"

She felt a strange sensation in the air around her.

Everyone had gone silent. They only stared at her, like she really was some monster.

"No, you're not," Bron said quickly. "Of course not."

His voice was so soothing...

She shook her head and felt the anger leave her. After a breath, she felt like herself again.

"Holy cow!" Sara said, seeming genuinely surprised. "You looked just like the fachan for a second. How did you do that?"

Miranda had no idea what she was talking about.

"No," Tabitha chimed in. "She looked just like that harpy we fought at the school."

"You can change your appearance," Dorian said, sounding impressed.

"No," Bron corrected him. "She didn't change what she looked like. She changed how we saw her."

Had she really done that?

Miranda took a deep, slow breath. Her power had never taken on this dimension. It had certainly never been anywhere near this strong. She hoped she could control it.

"This is insane," Tabitha said. "No offense, Miranda, but with that kind of power, and knowing where your loyalties lie, it's really hard for us to trust you."

"She helped us," Tristan said quietly. "Let it go for now, my queen."

Tabitha bit her lip, but allowed Tristan to lead her back up the path toward their cars.

"That really was amazing," Sara said brightly to Miranda. "I was falling and my feet just... *stopped*."

Miranda smiled grimly, but didn't answer. She didn't need to make Tabitha any angrier.

"Where did you learn to sing like that?" she asked instead.

"No idea," Sara told her. "I've always had this weird feeling when I sing, but it's grown stronger and stronger. Then Dorian came along and helped me realize I should use it instead of ignoring it."

Dorian smiled and Miranda was amazed to see the big man with the dark expression looking momentarily sunny.

"I'll go with the mortal for tonight," Bron said suddenly.

"Oh, we got the fachan. I'm sure I'll be fine," she said, though her heart beat a little faster at the idea of bringing him home again.

He scowled at her and then turned up his nose and marched ahead of them through the woods.

"He's not good at talking about his feelings," Sara confided softly. "But I think he really likes you."

Miranda smiled in spite of herself.

"I like him, too," she said. "But I think it's probably best for us all to keep our space from each other, given the circumstances."

Sara looked a little disappointed. But she brightened quickly.

"Did you know we have only two more monsters to catch?" she confided. "I kind of wish we had you around a little longer. It seems like we could wrap things up quickly with all of us assembled."

"Unfortunately, I've got to get back to work tomorrow," Miranda said. "My boss isn't prone to giving days off."

"If you change your mind, text me," Sara said, slipping Miranda a business card.

"Tarker's Hollow Realty Group?" Miranda read dubiously. "You're a real estate agent?"

"Guilty as charged," Sara replied happily. "Monster hunting is more of a side hustle."

Miranda laughed in spite of herself.

They had reached the parking lot.

"It was great to hunt monsters with you guys," Miranda said, meaning it.

Sara grinned and even Tabitha nodded her head in acknowledgement.

Tristan gave her a smile and Dorian waved.

Only Bron stood still as a statue in the light of the nearly full moon.

"Thank you for helping me, Bron," Miranda added softly.

He turned to her and she could see the pain and longing in his eyes.

He feels it too. This strange pull between us...

She spun on her heel and headed for her car, hopping in as fast as she could and taking off down the trail before she could change her mind.

She just needed a bath and a little sleep, she decided. She was not really mooning over some woodland fae king. Everything would seem normal again in the morning. She was sure of it.

6

———

MIRANDA

iranda awoke at dawn, beating the alarm on her phone to the punch, as usual.

The bed at the Inn was soft and cozy. She stretched and took a moment to look out the window at the blue Tarker's Hollow sky, her mind buzzing with unanswered questions.

In the bright daylight, last night didn't seem real at all.

Had she really changed how the others saw her?

Was something like that even possible?

Were there really monsters in the woods?

Did she really have the power to command them?

That last thought seemed the most unlikely of all. It had probably been part luck and partly the power of surprise.

Though Sara's words echoed in her head.

I was falling and my feet just… stopped.

Well, she was most likely never going to see any of them again, so it wasn't worth worrying about.

She'd stumbled back to the Inn last night drained and exhausted. Right now she felt like she could barely command herself to get out of bed.

She decided to take a hot shower and then hunt down some breakfast.

As the steaming water pounded down on her, she thought suddenly about how she'd felt last night, padding back to the bedroom of her suite in just a towel, past the burly fae king.

His eyes on her were a revelation, sending lightning bolts of awareness through her.

He probably had that effect on every woman - it was probably just part of being a king, or just part of looking like a walking nature god.

But of course, the other two kings, gorgeous, refined, and *so* much more her type as they were, had no such effect on her libido.

"Don't think about it," she advised herself. "You've got to get back to the city and focus on work."

But when she wandered back into the bedroom, wrapped in a fluffy hotel robe, and checked her phone there was a text from her boss waiting.

CULLEN WARD:

Don't bother coming in today. I've got a few things to take care of. Take a couple of days off. Enjoy.

SHE BLINKED and read it again.

Miranda had been working for Cullen Ward for almost three years.

In that time, he had never once given her an unplanned day off. Even when things were quiet, he always kept her close.

She wondered vaguely what in the world he needed to get done. Mr. Ward never took time off for himself, either.

She read the message a third time.

Nope, she hadn't imagined it.

She sat on the edge of the bed and wondered what she would actually do.

But she already knew.

She was up, grabbing Sara Mason's business card from the dresser, texting her before she could change her mind.

Miranda Cannon:

Hey, my boss just told me to take a couple of days off.

She put the phone down and went to get dressed.

It buzzed almost immediately.

Sara Mason:

Perfect! Meet me at Le Sucre in an hour. We'll make a plan. Bring a bathing suit if you have one

Miranda looked down at the phone.

It really was going to be that easy. Something about these people made her feel at home.

Though the bathing suit thing threw her a little.

Miranda Cannon:

Okay, see you then

. . .

SHE DRESSED in work clothes and headed out right away. Hopefully, the mall in Springton still had a decent plus size store. Miranda loved her strong body, but her height and curves could make it tough to shop for anything at the last minute.

The air outside was fragrant with the heavy blooms of the rose bushes that lined the eating area of the little tavern on the first floor of the Inn.

Miranda was feeling good as she got into her car and headed for Springton for a quick shopping trip.

An hour later, dressed in new casual clothing, and shoes that could handle a long walk in the woods, she arrived at Le Sucre.

Sara's little car was already outside.

"*I'm gonna take you by the hand and make you understand, Miranda,*" the barista sang loudly as she entered.

"What?" she asked.

"Sara told me your name," he replied. "But I cheated a little on the song lyrics."

She nodded, trying to keep up.

"Miranda, that's Carl," Sara yelled from what appeared to be her usual table up by the window.

Their last meeting here hadn't been so pleasant. She pushed the thoughts aside and focused on the present.

"Hey, Carl," Miranda said.

"Hey, yourself," he replied. "What can I fix you?"

She gave her order and then headed over to sit opposite Sara.

"So how much time do you have off?" Sara asked.

"I'm actually not sure," Miranda said.

"That seems kind of unusual," Sara said.

"It *is* unusual," Miranda replied thoughtfully. "I emailed

my boss yesterday afternoon and let him know about the worker who got hurt."

"You didn't tell him the monster was real, did you?" Sara whispered.

"Oh God, no," Miranda said. "I just told him what the workers told me. I sent that email from the cabin, before anything else happened. He probably thought it was as ridiculous as I did."

"I'm just selfishly glad there are three of us mortals in on it," Sara confided. "Otherwise I might think I was actually losing my mind."

"If you were just watching, maybe," Miranda allowed. "But you're *making* magic."

"Right back at you," Sara said. "Listen, I let Tabitha know you were coming, and she wants us to meet her at the museum after breakfast. Did you bring a bathing suit?"

Miranda tried not to show that she was disappointed.

"Don't worry about Tabitha. She'll come around," Sara said softly, as if reading her thoughts. "We've been best friends forever, and this whole magic thing was something just the two of us shared. But it's obvious to me that you're part of the circle now. Whatever is going on with your boss, we'll figure it out."

"He won't change his mind," Miranda said right away, not wanting to be dishonest.

"*There are stranger things on heaven and Earth, Horatio, than are dreamt of in your philosophy,*" Sara misquoted hopefully.

"Oh, a little Shakespeare with your breakfast, eh?" Carl asked as he carried over a tray covered in fruit and eggs. "Here you go, ladies. Enjoy!"

Miranda dug in and tried to take the advice everyone seemed to be giving her today and just enjoy herself. It wasn't hard to take satisfaction in a good meal with a new friend.

As long as she didn't allow herself to wonder why she was supposed to have a bathing suit with her for monster hunting, that was.

7

MIRANDA

iranda followed Sara and Tabitha through the parking lot of the Rosethorn Valley Swim Club, her flip-flops kicking up the gravel as they walked. She was beginning to wonder why it seemed like nothing in this town was paved.

"Okay, listen up, Miranda," Tabitha said in a very businesslike way for someone wearing a polka-dotted terrycloth coverup and a pair of cat eye sunglasses.

At least Miranda was finally going to hear the plan.

"The pieces of the mirror show us the view from the monsters. We haven't seen much activity in the last two shards, but late last night we saw something that looked a lot like this area," Tabitha said. "So we're going to enjoy a day at the pool, while surreptitiously checking it out."

"Nice," Miranda said.

"A couple of ground rules," Tabitha said. "First of all, discretion is key here. Secondly, you can't tell people who you are. If someone recognizes you, we're out of luck. Rosethorn Valley protects its own. As far as anyone knows, you're just a friend out from the city. Got it?"

"You know I'm from the town next door, right?" Miranda asked. "I've been to this pool before. Chances are pretty good someone here will know me."

"Let's hope not," Tabitha told her. "It will be much easier for us to lay low if people aren't wondering why we're hanging out together."

Miranda was beginning to wonder exactly why they *were* hanging out together.

But she had to admit that Tabitha had a point, so she nodded instead.

"Good," Tabitha said. "Let's keep a sharp eye out for anything out of place."

"We've sure got a beautiful day for it," Sara said.

She was right. The sky was deep blue above, without a cloud in sight. The birds were singing, and the tall trees that surrounded the little club were so lush, they almost looked tropical.

They headed through the gates to the little booth by the pool where Tabitha turned in her membership card and signed for two guests.

Miranda had been here once or twice over the years for swap days and birthday parties. As a kid, she'd belonged to the neighboring Tarker's Hollow swim club, which was wide open, with huge pools, slides, swing sets and a massive campus.

But this place was very different.

Rosethorn Valley's swim club was like a hidden gem, its smaller pools and tennis court tucked away in the tiny valley between the creek and the cliffside.

The creek itself was very much a part of the place. It ran parallel to the pools, with little bridges leading between the tennis court and pool and to the stone steps carved into the hillside that led to the changing rooms.

Massive trees on the hills that surrounded the place made the pool feel sheltered, but also guaranteed that the water was iceberg cold during most of the day.

Miranda followed Tabitha and Sara as they headed past a collection of Rosethorn Valley's senior citizens, who were sunning themselves on lawn chairs around the deep end of the biggest pool.

Sara threw her bag on one of the picnic tables and sat down to put on sunscreen.

"Can I borrow some of that?" Miranda asked.

"Sure," Sara said, handing it over.

Miranda slathered on a healthy amount. Her fair skin had always been super sensitive.

"Are we looking for anything in particular?" she asked.

"We couldn't see much," Sara said. "But I caught a glimpse of the stone stairs over there. At least I think it was them. We really have so little to go on."

"Let's swim first," Tabitha suggested. "It will clear our minds."

"Sounds good," Miranda said.

They headed over to the crystal-clear water.

Tabitha dove right in, barely making a splash, and began swimming laps.

Sara stepped in gingerly and quickly went under, coming up with a little yelp. "It's so cold," she said, with a sheepish expression.

Miranda braced herself and dipped in a toe.

"Dear Lord," she muttered.

But there was no point delaying the inevitable. It would be better to freeze than to sweat.

She stepped down and slid underwater.

The cold invaded her body, momentarily taking her breath away. She shivered once, then began to adjust.

"Invigorating, right?" Tabitha said enthusiastically, already finished with her first lap.

"Sure," Miranda agreed, earning herself a genuine smile from the other woman.

"Come on, let's get our exercise," Tabitha said. "The guys are coming later with a ton of food."

"Sounds good to me," Miranda said.

They swam laps for a while in the late morning sunshine.

It had been forever since Miranda had gotten exercise that wasn't meted out by a machine in a stale indoor gym. The pull and stretch of her muscles in the cold water felt amazing.

When she got tired, she flipped over and did a lazy backstroke.

The tall trees put a border around the blue sky above and Miranda had the same sense of happy quiet she used to feel as a child, walking around Tarker's Hollow under the tree canopy.

A sort of benevolent magic seemed to protect this place from too many dark days. It was an abomination to think of monsters invading, stealing away its ephemeral peace.

"Oh boy, here they come," Sara said, rousing Miranda from this train of thought.

She righted herself in time to see the three fae kings striding toward the pool.

Separately, they were each magnificent.

Together, they were a revelation.

The sun had just reached the pinnacle of the sky, shining its rays at last on the glittering water and burnishing the men as if the sun itself admired them. They were all lean muscle and long hair, smiles and easy confidence.

Miranda felt like she was watching a commercial, but for

what she could not imagine. Not that any product would have a chance at holding anyone's attention with them in the frame. The men were beautiful and larger than life.

The older ladies around the deep end were unabashedly lowering their sunglasses to have a look, and the whole Rosethorn Valley Swim Club seemed to hold its breath as one.

"Hello, Miranda," Bron called out in his deep voice.

The ladies around the pool let out their collective breath in a sigh.

Miranda gave a little wave.

Bron beamed at her.

Tabitha and Sara headed out of the pool and back to the umbrella-shaded picnic table, where the guys were already unpacking items from bags and a cooler.

Miranda followed them. By the time she arrived, the whole surface of the table was covered in packages of hot dogs, hamburgers, and buns, as well as every conceivable spread and sauce imaginable, including Worcestershire sauce, pico de gallo and marshmallow fluff.

"Wow, you guys really went all out," Tabitha said, arching an eyebrow.

"We were both hungry and curious," Tristan replied.

Tabitha smiled up at him and Miranda could see the love they shared was even warmer than the midday sun.

Dorian had an arm around Sara's shoulder as they surveyed the varieties of hot dogs to find the right one to grill first.

Miranda felt a pang of aching loneliness.

"Which of these do you like best?" Bron asked, placing a hand on her shoulder.

His warm touch sent a shiver of awareness through her.

"Oh, uh, I love a good burger," she said.

"Me too," he chuckled. "That's one thing you get right in this realm."

She couldn't resist glancing up at him.

His green eyes danced as he smiled down at her.

She thought maybe he'd be vegetarian, since he was so into protecting nature. But one glance at his muscular physique was enough to make her forget about that idea. You didn't get a body like that from kale smoothies.

"Shall we fire up the grill?" Dorian asked, looking uncharacteristically cheerful.

"Let's do it," Sara replied.

The process of cooking was drawn-out. The kings were very interested in the grill, but impatient with their own limited abilities, which ultimately led to more than one hot dog bun fight.

As the first of the meals came off the grill, she thought that pretty much the entire population of the kiddie pool had crowded around to see what shenanigans would happen next.

Bron offered meals to the kids and Miranda was shocked to find that the parents around the pool weren't a bit taken aback. They all waved their kids on to take food from these enormous, boisterous strangers.

By the time the six friends were sitting down at their own picnic table again, half the people at the pool were eating the food the fae kings had shared. Some had even politely added the weird extras to their burgers and dogs.

"This is delicious," Tristan decided. He was eating a burger that, as far as Miranda could tell, was just a bun full of pickles.

"The fluff is very sticky," Dorian complained, scowling at his burger.

"I told you not to use so much of it," Sara scolded. "A little bit goes a long way."

"Well, I think the pico is great on a hotdog personally," Tabitha said. "Miranda?"

"Delicious," Miranda agreed.

Everything about the day had been delicious.

They all got back in the pool for a game of volleyball with some of the other swimmers. And for a while, Miranda didn't think about work, or monsters, or out of control magical powers.

For a few hours, Miranda just had fun.

8

MIRANDA

Miranda packed up her things as the crowd at the pool dispersed.

The sun was setting, and there had been no sign of anything out of the ordinary. She guessed that made the day count as a loss for them, but somehow it didn't feel that way. Miranda thought she'd actually gained quite a bit. For the first time in a long time, she had spent more time talking to real friends instead of buried in her work.

She dreaded the number of messages that must surely be waiting for her, but she was determined not to think about that until she had to.

Just then, a tinkly song began to play, breaking her out of her thoughts.

"Oh my God, the ice cream truck," Sara breathed.

"Does anyone have any cash?" Tabitha asked, sounding panicky.

"No," Sara moaned.

"I do," Miranda said, grabbing her bag. "Come on."

They dashed past the lap pool.

"No running," a young male lifeguard called out to them.

They slowed to a speed-walk, and made it across the little bridge over the creek and back to the parking lot as quickly as they could.

Miranda pulled a wad of cash out of her wallet.

"I'm really glad you're here," Tabitha said, putting a hand on her wrist.

"You just want ice cream," Miranda teased.

"Well, yes," Tabitha admitted. "But seriously, it's been a nice day. Thanks for deciding to help us."

"My pleasure," Miranda replied, feeling more relieved at the gesture of acceptance than she would have thought possible.

They let all the little kids go in front of them while the men checked out the pictured offerings on the side of the truck. Then they all chose their treats and headed back to the pool at a leisurely pace.

The sun had sunk below the hillside and the sky over the pools was painted a beautiful pink.

Sara and Tabitha were deep in a discussion with Tristan and Dorian about something going on at the museum.

Miranda found herself hanging back to admire the blooming rhododendrons on the hillside.

"They're very hardy," Bron said approvingly.

She turned to find him looking over her shoulder at the rhododendrons.

"And they're travelers," he told her.

"How?" she asked, wondering how something with roots in the ground could travel.

"Look," he told her, gesturing toward the hillside, where an army of rhodies stretched up toward the cottages on the twilit hillside above.

"Each plant expands," he told her. "Eventually, they move together to form their own jungle."

"I guess it's just a matter of watching them over time," Miranda said thoughtfully. "Even if you can't actually see them moving."

"Time moves differently for me," he murmured, gazing fondly at the rhododendron. "I can see her moving if I choose."

The idea was incredible to Miranda.

She wondered what she would do with her time if it were limitless. Would she still be constantly on the go, or would she find the time to sit and watch flowers bloom?

"Careful," Bron said, moving close.

Her own time did seem to slow as he reached out his hand to touch her face.

Miranda felt the warmth of his rough thumb against her mouth.

He leaned closer still and pulled his thumb back to his tongue, tasting the drop of ice cream she realized he had scooped from her lips.

Blood rushed to her cheeks and she was suddenly aware of every cell in her body, reaching, straining toward the King of the Wilds.

A whistle sounded and she nearly jumped.

"That means the pool is closing," Bron said sadly.

"I guess we should go finish packing up," she said.

As they made their way past the lifeguard station where they'd been yelled at for running, Miranda overheard a young female lifeguard muttering to herself.

"I can't believe he just left," the girl said. "Didn't bother to clean up the pool noodles. Didn't even turn in his whistle."

Something about that struck her as odd. The lifeguards

at these local pools were mostly students who took the job very seriously. It was a coveted opportunity.

Leaving without checking out would have been unheard of back in Miranda's day. Maybe things had changed.

She walked over to where Sara and Tabitha were divvying up the leftover sauces as Dorian and Tristan folded towels and stuffed them into beach bags.

"Did anyone see anything at all today?" Miranda asked Tabitha.

Tabitha shook her head. "I guess it wasn't here. Or at least it isn't here now."

They had walked past the lap pool and were headed for the bridge when another lifeguard came jogging in from the parking lot.

"His car is still here," she yelled.

Tabitha and Miranda exchanged a glance.

"So where is he, then?" the other lifeguard called back.

"Who knows?" the first one yelled. "He said something about fireflies earlier. Maybe he went for a walk."

"Will o' the wisps," Sara whispered to Tabitha, stopping in her tracks.

"Sorry, folks, we're closing up," one of the lifeguards told them.

"Oh, of course," Sara said.

"Sorry," Miranda added.

They headed for the parking lot.

"We'll move the cars and then walk back in and hide in the tennis court before they lock up," Tabitha whispered.

Miranda nodded and they marched off en masse.

It was only when they reached her car that she realized she was willingly going along with an evening of breaking and entering to look for a monster in the dark woods.

All while wearing a bathing suit.

This was not how she thought her day was going to end up.

But when Bron smiled down at her as he opened the car door, her doubts faded away and she was filled instead with excitement at being part of an amazing adventure, and a steadfast determination to find the young lifeguard who was missing.

"Let's do this," she said, and Bron gave her a wink that made her insides do a little flip-flop.

9

BRON

Bron's heart pounded and he struggled for control.

Whatever was happening with Miranda, it was driving him mad.

He was beginning to realize he wanted more than to bed her, but he couldn't imagine what more there could be for them.

She's mortal, she's mortal, she's mortal...

But it didn't seem to matter. He adored her. She was as sweet as ice cream, and the idea of seeing her in danger again terrified him.

It certainly hadn't mattered for his brothers.

"Get in, Bron," Dorian hissed from the passenger side of Sara's car.

"I'm going with Miranda," he decided.

She nodded and he moved around and got in beside her.

"Do you think the lifeguard is in danger?" Miranda asked.

By the gods, he did not want to admit his fear, but the folk could not lie.

"It is impossible for us to know for sure," he told her.

She glanced at him.

"But yes," he admitted. "I do think he's in danger. It will be good if we can get back there quickly and try to find him."

"Good idea," she said, nodding.

She was very brave. Injury at the hands of one of these monsters could be fatal to her. Yet she was ready to fling herself into danger to save someone she didn't know, and help people she had just met.

"Hopefully, we can find it quickly," she said. "Do you have an advantage? Being... who you are?"

"That depends," he told her. "All living things are known at least a little bit to me. But it is the simpler side of nature that is most mine. Plants, animals, and... other simple creatures."

"You were going to say humans, weren't you?" He could see the little dimple on her right cheek. She wasn't angry.

"Yes," he admitted. "Though you are not entirely under my rule."

"That's good news," she said, quirking an eyebrow.

"Your kind has more complexity, generally," he said.

"But not always?"

"Not always," he agreed.

She was silent and he could hear her unasked question hanging between them.

"You are more complex, Miranda Cannon," he told her gruffly. "You do not belong to me wholly."

Not yet.

"But I do a little bit?" she asked.

He wasn't sure whether she thought that was a good or a bad thing. But he had no time to puzzle it out. She was pulling the car over behind Sara's.

They got out and joined their friends.

"This way," Tabitha said, heading for a ditch on the edge of the road.

"Are you sure?" Sara asked.

"I used to sneak into the pool sometimes in high school," Tabitha said over her shoulder.

Sara's eyes widened and Miranda tried to hide her smile under her hand.

"What is funny?" Bron whispered to Miranda as they followed Tabitha into the ditch.

"Even in Tarker's Hollow I knew all about the Barnes family," she whispered. "They're kind of... proper. It seems wild that Tabitha ever snuck into a pool."

"Tabitha is not proper," Bron informed her. "At least not in the way you're thinking."

"I'm starting to get that," Miranda admitted.

They stepped out of the ditch and into the woods and the trees closed in all around them.

Bron took in a deep breath of the rich air. He was learning to appreciate his own realm more in this strange place where the sounds and scents of nature were often missing or covered with chemicals.

Tabitha led the way and Bron brought up the rear.

He kept his eyes on Miranda, who was just in front of him. Though he told himself he was merely making sure she didn't fall behind, his need to protect her was something much more than that.

He felt a sort of mournful admiration for the human woman, a feeling that he had never experienced so acutely before.

His brothers' queens were mortal too, but to him that felt inevitable. They were as they had been made.

But this woman, who was so like him in stature and

coloring, every moment with her felt both beautiful and tragic.

"Okay, here we go," Tabitha whispered, slipping through a break in the fence.

Tristan had a decidedly harder time fitting through after her, but he held the material back to help the others.

"Well done, brother," Bron told him on his way through.

Tristan nodded.

There was an easy accord between the brothers now. Bron had not known this ease in the faerie realm, and he certainly wouldn't have expected it, not after they had all stood by and watched Dorian's imprisonment without lifting a finger to help him.

Perhaps it was his weakness for the mortal woman, but Bron suddenly had a much better understanding of his brother's sympathy for these creatures.

Though he knew it was wrong to harbor such mischief in a court of good, he also knew his brother's heart. Darkness was Dorian's realm, but he was kind. His actions hadn't been meant to harm.

By the time they reached the pool again, Bron was lost in thought and their sudden arrival took him by surprise. He realized they had approached from behind the snack shack, on the other side of the lap pool from the entrance.

Tabitha gestured for everyone to wait.

She and Tristan slipped around the side of the shack as Dorian drew dark shadows around them.

A moment later, they reappeared.

"No one seems to have stayed around," Tabitha said. "They must have decided he left with someone else."

"What do we do?" Sara asked.

"They said he saw fireflies," Dorian said. "I'm guessing that was the wisps trying to lead him away."

They looked around. There weren't many places he could have been led to. The three pools glimmered in the moonlight. A fence surrounded the whole area, except where the creek flowed freely through the valley.

"The creek," Sara murmured.

"That's why we saw the changing room walls from that angle," Tabitha said, her eyes brightening. "It was from the perspective of the creek, not the pool."

They moved to the creek and walked along its bank, past the lap pool, the medium sized pool, and the one for mortal babies.

There was nothing unusual about the water - it burbled pleasantly along in its pebbly bed.

"Look," Miranda said, pointing ahead of them.

Twinkling lights had appeared at the place where the creek moved through the break in the fence.

"Let's follow them," Sara suggested. "I can catch the wisps when they've led us to our quarry."

They all murmured assent and the kept moving.

When they reached the break, Tristan leapt over the fence and Dorian handed him Sara, then Tabitha.

Bron felt a twinge of jealousy at the idea that his brothers would handle the mortal he was growing close with.

But when she reached the fence-break Miranda held back.

"Come, Miranda," Dorian said.

"I'll climb over myself," she said.

"It's too high," he said.

"I-I'm too big," she said. "I'd rather just climb it myself."

Bron could practically hear her blush.

He strode up. "I've got you," he offered.

Bron was physically bigger than his brothers, a fact they

had often exploited when playing hide and seek as children. The two of them would squeeze themselves into tight spots where Bron couldn't follow.

Tonight he was glad his size was such that this mortal woman could not possibly think herself too large for him to handle.

She sighed and lifted her arms.

He picked her up gently and handed her over to Tristan, who lowered her gracefully to the ground.

By the time Bron and Dorian reached the other side of the fence, Miranda was smiling at him.

He smiled back, feeling like a garden in springtime, buds exploding with riotous color in his soul.

"Shh," Tristan warned them, indicating the way forward.

In the distance, tiny lights were twinkling over the creek.

They made their way along the bank as quietly as they could. They followed the creek around a slight curve to a place where it widened to a small pond.

Sara gasped at the sight of two figures, standing on the bank.

One was the lifeguard, young and reasonably hand-some, his face awestruck, his big, puppyish hand extended.

The other was a beautiful, coal-black horse.

It stood easily thirty hands tall, thick muscles rippling under a satiny coat that gleamed in the light of the moon. Its long, shining mane lifted slightly in the summer breeze, and the hair of its tail and fluffy fetlocks moved in tandem so that the horse appeared to be moving, even though it wasn't. Between the lift of its fur and the dappled moonlight from the trees above, it almost looked like it was...

Underwater.

"No," Bron roared.

But it was too late.

The boy's hand touched the velvety nose of the sinister steed and in a heartbeat, he was being pulled inexorably into the water.

The creature was no horse. It was a kelpie.

And kelpies lived to drown.

They drowned animals and ate them.

They drowned mortals and ate them.

They drowned other fae creatures just to watch them struggle and soundlessly scream.

And now this young boy was going to die in the cold water if something wasn't done.

Before Bron could even decide what to do, he saw Miranda move. She sprinted toward the boy, singular in her purpose.

She had known what that kelpie was by instinct, though Bron knew she couldn't name what it was.

As the inky horse pulled the boy under, Miranda dove in after them, her body pale against the black water.

"Miranda," Bron cried, his voice breaking as he ran after her.

Dorian was calling midnight now, shadows gathering over his dark head, swirling over the creek to blot out the moonlight.

Sara held out the mirror in quivering hands as Tabitha followed Miranda into the depths.

Bron dove in. Even though it was full summer, the water was so cold he thought it might stop his heart.

Instantly, he felt the presence of the algae and fish that called this place their home. Their universe was awash in activity and they sensed the inherent wrongness of the kelpie.

Pushing their bubbling fretfulness aside, Bron reached out with his mind for Miranda and found her struggling.

She was somewhere on the rocky bottom of this pond, hooves holding her down as the kelpie raged against her for trying to steal its prey.

Bron moved toward them, feeling for the boy.

A grassy green energy tinged the water where the young one thrashed.

"Easy," Bron murmured when he felt warm flesh against his hand.

He could feel the kelpie now. It was not really a horse, or he could have communicated with it easily. Its energy was pinched and wild.

He placed a hand on its muscular neck and managed to cling on to the rough mane.

"*Easy,*" he said again, trying to reach the part of it that was a horse.

It stilled for an instant and he heard Miranda and the boy both break the surface of the water.

The boy scrambled instantly for the bank, where Sara and Tabitha pulled him up.

"Are you okay?" Bron heard Sara ask.

The boy ran into the trees, presumably back to his car and home.

"Easy," Bron told the kelpie again.

It tossed its head and he could see the whites of its eyes.

"Easy," Miranda whispered from the other side of the beast.

Bron noticed that her hand was on its sleek neck, same as his.

She was echoing his words and commands.

And it was working.

Between his command of the horse nature of the beast and her ability to compel creatures with her words, they were holding the thing still.

"*Now*, Sara," Tabitha said quietly, realizing they had a small window of opportunity.

GORGEOUS HUNTER OF THE SEA,
  Mouth so hungry, hooves so free,
  You came here to find new prey,
  Shallow water stole it away,
  Empty belly, you need more,
  Hunt no more upon this shore,
  Back to your home and waters deep
  With prey to chase and souls to keep
  Flimsy boats, prey at the helm,
  Are back inside your mirror realm.

SARA CLOSED HER EYES.

Bron felt huge muscles move in slow motion under his hands.

The kelpie leapt bonelessly out of the water and disappeared into the mirror shard in Sara's hands as Dorian bound the veil of midnight tightly around them.

An instant later, it was done.

Sara held the mirror, an amazed look on her face.

"Where's Tristan?" Tabitha asked.

They looked around.

"There," Dorian said, pointing past the inlet.

Tristan stood in the distance. Light emanated from his whole body.

The Will o' the wisps surrounded him like stars in a galaxy.

Sara took off toward him, digging in her bag for the last mirror shard.

Dorian was right behind her, midnight trailing behind him like a cloak.

"Are you okay?" Bron asked Miranda.

"I'm fine," she gasped. "We should help them."

"No, love," he told her, holding her close. "The wisps have nothing left to lure travelers to. They'll give up without a fight."

She relaxed slightly in his arms and he became aware of the warmth blossoming between them.

"You're crazy," he murmured into her hair. "You could have died."

"The boy was in trouble," she said. "I can take care of myself."

And he loved her for her pluck, even though she had clearly been on the creek bed being trampled and drowned when he'd found her.

"I was glad to see you though," she admitted.

He threw his head back and laughed.

Beyond them, he could hear Sara singing to the wisps, drawing them into their shard.

"I guess that's it," Miranda said softly. "No more monsters."

He heard what she was saying, and knew what it meant. There was no more reason for them to spend time together.

He felt as if the garden in his soul were withering.

The others cheered as they all headed down the bank.

"We still have to return the shards to the mirror," he told her. "You'll come with us for that. You're the only one who is legally allowed to be there."

"Sure," she said, looking chastened. "Of course."

"I didn't mean—" he began.

"It's fine," she said lightly.

"Ready to head to the mansion?" Sara asked excitedly as the others joined them.

"Sure," Bron said. "Miranda is coming, too."

"Of course she is," Tabitha said, marching past him to grab Miranda by the arm and drag her back toward the pool.

"We did it, brothers," Tristan said brightly.

It was good to see Tristan looking so happy. For all that he was the King of Light, he had always been sullen. Not so much anymore. Bron suspected it was Tabitha's effect on him.

Dorian clapped a hand on Bron's shoulder.

"She's lovely," Dorian said.

"Who?" Bron asked.

Dorian let out a barking laugh and Bron almost tripped he was so surprised.

"Having a queen suits your humor, brother," Bron said.

"You should try it," Dorian told him.

"They're mortal," Bron said, wishing he understood why they were so drawn to these short-lived women. "What will you do when she's gone?"

"No idea," Dorian said. "To be honest, I can't picture it at all. I'm just trying to enjoy what we have for as long as we have it."

"But she puts herself in danger," Bron said. "How can you let her chase these monsters?"

"She's good at it, and it makes her happy," Dorian said. "Who am I to stop her?"

"You're the bloody King of Darkness," Bron retorted.

"Before her, I was a pauper," Dorian said with a strange half-smile.

Bron observed his brother in wonder.

But Dorian only walked on, past the pools and through the fence to join his queen.

His queen...

Was that the feeling that was drawing him to Miranda?

Bron pushed the bothersome thought aside and ran to join his brothers.

10

MIRANDA

iranda followed the others into the mansion on the cliffside.

Bron had been silent in the car the whole way over.

She wasn't sure if she had done something wrong, or if he was merely pensive. She didn't really blame him. After all, this was the end of their adventure.

The six of them stepped up onto the porch without speaking, all of them perhaps awed at the magnitude of what they were about to do.

Tristan stepped forward, cupping the padlock that hung from the door in his hand.

It sprung open with a click.

He turned the knob and the door swung inward to reveal the interior of the empty mansion.

Miranda had been here before, but only during the day. The place was kind of cool but also depressing with its nests of cobwebs and old furniture standing silently like mourners at a funeral.

In the darkness, the dust disappeared and she saw only

the elegant lines of the curved staircase and the moonlight on the black and white tiles of the foyer.

"Come on," Sara whispered.

They headed into the conservatory.

A huge section was missing from the mirror on the wall. This was the part that had been smashed when Sara released Dorian and the monsters.

Sara crouched on the floor, pulling shards out of her bag and lining them up in order.

"There," she said in satisfaction.

Sure enough, the pieces on the floor fit together like a puzzle, in the exact shape of the missing section on the wall.

Tabitha pulled out a roll of duct tape and they worked together to stick the pieces in place.

When they were finished, the mirror was whole once more, with cracks outlining each shard.

"Tabitha," Tristan said quietly, holding a fog of warm, soft light between his palms.

Instantly, Miranda felt peace in her soul. She wondered if Tristan was using his powers to lend confidence to his queen.

Tabitha extended her hands to touch the mirror as Dorian pulled the shadows down around them all.

Miranda felt a tremor, as if the whole house were holding its breath.

But nothing happened. Scars still rent the mirror.

"I don't understand," Tabitha said.

"Try again," Tristan encouraged her.

They all focused their energies and the room filled with shadows once more.

When Dorian lifted the darkness again, the mirror was the same.

"I can't restore it," Tabitha said, shaking her head. "It's not ready to come together."

"Oh," Sara said. "The corner."

"Of course," Tabitha said, turning one of the mounts that held the mirror in place to reveal another missing piece. "We noticed this piece was missing before Sara broke the rest of it. I didn't even think about it. But it feels like that's what's holding it from going back together. It wants to be whole."

"But you said each shard was a creature," Miranda said. "So if a piece is missing, does that mean…"

"Something is loose, and has been," Bron said. "Something that was already here in the realm before Sara freed Dorian and the other creatures."

"That's impossible," Sara said. "If there were a monster, we'd know it."

Her words hung in the air.

Miranda moved to look at the broken corner of the mirror.

There was something about it, something about the shape, it was almost familiar…

Oh, God…

She had seen it before.

It shouldn't have been possible, but she was sure of it.

"I-I have to check my email," she yelped, and dashed from the room.

Even the soaring ceiling of the foyer felt like it was closing in.

Miranda dashed outside, off the covered porch and into the rose garden, where moonlight turned the flowers a deep indigo.

Out of the looming shadow of that horrid house, Miranda felt like she could breathe again.

She closed her eyes and pictured the mirror shard. Maybe she had been wrong about it...

But in her mind's eye it was right there. She allowed herself to go back to the time when she'd seen it.

Mr. Ward had asked her to accompany him to retrieve a special pen from a private lockbox. It was protected by three layers of security. A personal guard stood on duty outside his office at all times. The door to the office could only be opened through a biometric lock that responded to Cullen Ward's handprint. And finally, the box was tucked away in a secret space behind a false closet that was secured by an optic scanner attuned to her boss's face.

When at last they reached the box after jumping through all those hoops, Miranda had expected it to be filled with riches like diamonds, cash, and paper stocks.

Instead, it contained only a few seemingly mundane items. A soft folded pink fabric that looked like a woman's sweater covered the bottom of the box. On top of it were a tattered paperback book, a leather-bound journal, the pen he'd been seeking, and in the very back, like an afterthought, an irregular, palm-sized section of mirrored glass. The odd shape had caught her eye at the time, but she hadn't thought anything more of it until she saw that exact same shape just a few minutes ago - missing from the huge mirror in the old mansion.

Is my boss mixed up with some kind of fae monster?

But she knew the real answer without having to think about it.

Cullen Ward was a big man, bigger than any she had met before she encountered the fae kings. His shirt had even fit Bron.

Miranda knew big men tended to do well in business. But Mr. Ward was more than big. He was larger than life.

And it wasn't just his body, it was his presence and the way he held employees and investors in his thrall. There was definitely something more to him.

"Miranda," Bron called from the porch.

What am I supposed to do?

Cullen Ward had hired her right out of high school. Because of him she had a fat bank account, a portfolio of company stock, a beautiful downtown condo, and a list of personal contacts that would make any CEO drool.

Despite his reputation as a ruthless businessman, Mr. Ward had never been anything but kind to Miranda. And unlike other women she knew who had worked for powerful men like Ward, she had never been the victim of unwanted advances from him.

Surely, she was mistaken about this.

She slipped her phone out of her pocket and dashed off a quick email.

MR. WARD,

WHEN YOU HAVE A MOMENT, *could we meet up in person? There's something I need to ask you about.*

-*Miranda*

"MIRANDA," Bron called out again.

She slipped her phone back in her pocket and waved to him.

"I'm out here," she called.

His expression of relief gave her a pang of guilt.

Should I have told them?

But she didn't know anything for sure, at least not yet. It would be wrong to throw her boss under the bus for no reason.

Even if it meant keeping her friends in the dark.

11

BRON

Bron jogged down into the rose garden to join Miranda.

She smiled at him, but her smile was strange and sad.

It had been a long day, and their work was not yet complete. She was probably just tired - mortals felt the need for sleep more keenly than his kind.

But her worried expression told him there was something more.

"Hi," he said, feeling foolish as a boy in her presence.

"Hi," she replied, looking down.

"Is everything okay?" he asked.

"Sure," she said. "I mean, it's scary about the mirror."

She was simply frightened.

He felt a wave of relief. This was something he could help her with. He was sure of it.

"I will stay with you until that mirror is whole again," he told her.

"You don't have to do that," she told him. "I know you don't like the Inn."

"You could stay with me instead," he offered.

"Where do you live?" she asked.

"Wherever I want," he chuckled.

"Seriously?" she asked.

"Sure," he said. "Why not?"

"Like... camping?" Her expression of curiosity was adorable.

He was so glad that she didn't look sad or frightened anymore.

"A little like camping," he told her. "Want to give it a try? If you don't like it, I'll take you back to the Inn."

"Are you coming?" Dorian yelled from the parking area.

"We're going to stick around for a bit," Bron called back. "We'll see you guys tomorrow."

The others waved and Bron waved back.

"You guys are so close," Miranda observed. "It must be nice to have siblings."

Bron laughed. "Back in our own realm we were not always close."

He strode around the garden, looking for a spot that was wild enough to satisfy him but where she would feel at peace.

"What do you mean?" she asked, following him.

"We did not begin our lives as siblings," he said. "We were born to different families, and only taken in to be raised together because of our abilities. It is our shared upbringing that makes us brothers, not some accident of blood."

"I get that," she said, nodding. "I was adopted, too. And I'd never think of anyone else as my family. It always made me feel special to know that I was chosen."

That made sense. Maybe it was another reason he felt so close to her.

"But our childhood was not for childish games," he explained. "We were training to be powerful rulers. Our bonding was not encouraged. And at some point, we became truly independent, even turning our backs on each other in times of need, as we had been taught."

"Your parents didn't want you to get along with your brothers?" She sounded horrified.

"It's different for my kind," he said, shrugging. "But I am glad to be back among them. We are stronger together."

"Were you lonely," she asked. "During your time apart?"

"Oh no," he smiled. "I had the forest."

"Is it different in your world?" she asked,

"Yes," he told her. "There the forest is deeper, richer, more lush. At least I think so."

"What do you mean?" she asked.

"I have been asleep for so long," he said. "I'm not sure what it's like now."

He tried not to think about this part, but it was frightening to wonder what had happened in the fae realm since he had been gone.

"You were really just... asleep?" Miranda asked.

"Easy compared to what Dorian endured, right?" Bron asked.

"I don't know," Miranda said. "Was it?"

Bron shrugged and continued his search of the grounds.

It was hard closing your eyes in one time and waking up in another, especially when you were overly fond of natural things. Almost every plant and animal he had loved in Faerie was dead or dying by now.

The forest was new after every spring, with new saplings and baby animals to learn of and cherish.

But after this length of time, the forests of Faerie would be unrecognizable.

"What are we looking for?" Miranda asked.

"A good spot," he said. "And I think this is it."

It was a corner of the rose garden that was sheltered on three sides by a stone retaining wall.

"Yes," he decided. "It's perfect. Come sit with me."

She smiled and came to him, as if it would never occur to her not to do as he asked.

They sat on the grassy floor of the garden and he called the roses to him.

There was a rustling sound, like a breeze in the leaves, and then the branches began to move around them, forming a dome over their heads.

Miranda gasped.

"It's alright," Bron told her quietly. "They're making a shelter for us."

A small rabbit, who had been hiding among the roses, hopped softly over to them and curled itself in one of his hands.

"You're okay too, rabbit," Bron told it tenderly.

It gazed up at him, nose twitching curiously.

"He's not afraid of you," Miranda murmured.

"He is one of my subjects," Bron told her.

Miranda smiled and reached her hand out slowly.

She is ours, he told the creature with his mind.

The bunny stilled and allowed himself to be caressed by Miranda's trembling fingers.

The branches were weaving around them now, leaving Miranda and Bron in a snug little warren with a few small openings in the ceiling for moonlight to enter.

The rabbit hopped out of his hands and disappeared before they were completely enclosed.

"Wow," Miranda said. "So you meant what you said. You really can stay wherever you like."

"So long as my subjects are near, yes," he told her.

He observed her in the near-darkness.

Her heart rate was steady, and her eyes gleamed with interest.

For all her fancy clothing and just-right hair, this woman was ready for adventure and new experiences.

"You are incredible," she told him. "I've never met anyone like you."

"Let me see your hand," he heard himself say.

She slowly raised it, and he placed his palm against hers.

A shaft of moonlight illuminated their hands and allowed him to see the exact moment that inky vines appeared around their fingers, twining them together.

Miranda met his gaze, and in her eyes, he saw his own feelings reflected - fear, joy, and surprise.

But most of all, he saw her desire.

It was easy to recognize. He had felt it himself since the first moment he'd laid eyes on her.

"Bron," she whispered.

He pressed his lips to hers, tired of bucking his fate.

She kissed him back, bravely, as she did everything else.

A wave of lust washed over him, leaving him breathless.

He cupped her cheek in his hand and begged himself to go slowly. This wasn't some bawdy fae consort. This was a mortal woman, delicate in spite of her courage.

But when she moaned against his mouth, he began to lose his resolve.

He thumbed open her jaw and tasted her tongue as her arms went around his neck.

Her taste was pure sweetness, and her body was soft against his, melting into him as he kissed her, trying to imbibe her.

He could feel her desire as if it were his own.

She was of his realm.

He had not known it could be like this, her desire stoking his, the raw need echoing back and forth between them.

This was why they had kept him from mortals. The feeling was intoxicating. He never wanted to do anything else again but kiss this mortal woman and feel her need for him electrify them both.

But it wasn't enough, he needed more, and he knew she did, too.

He wrapped his arms around her and eased them both down to the soft grass. Miranda pressed herself closer to him, as if she wanted to meld her flesh to his.

He buried his face in her neck, inhaling her clean scent and nibbling her sensitive skin.

Miranda giggled, like a bubbling stream, and he drank in the sound.

He moved lower, sliding his thumbs under the straps of her swimming garment. She wiggled, helping him remove the thing completely, so that she lay naked beneath him.

He took in her pale, curving form for a moment, listening to the emotions that washed over her at once: desire, excitement, and embarrassment.

"You are everything a king could wish for in his queen," he told her gruffly, horrified that embarrassment could find its way into their joy.

He could sense the blood rushing to her cheeks, feel her smiling before he saw it.

She lifted her arms, urging him into her embrace.

But he needed to taste every inch of her first.

He lowered himself to her breasts, eager to hear the sounds she would make when he applied himself to her properly.

For a moment, all of their differences ceased to matter, and he lost himself in the desire that united them.

12

MIRANDA

Miranda nearly screamed with the pleasure of Bron's mouth on her skin.

Somehow, he knew before she did exactly what she needed, exactly what would make her shiver.

Somewhere in the back of her mind, an internal accountant was adding up the fact that a tattoo had just appeared around their fingers, that she was now inexorably connected with this wild man.

But she just couldn't bring herself to be upset about it.

Not when he was pressing kisses to her belly and thighs, nudging her legs apart to get to her sex.

"Miranda," he moaned, and she could hear what was unsaid in every harmonic of his gorgeous voice.

I love you.

I need you.

You are mine.

She let him have his way, parting her thighs wantonly, angling her hips to make it easy for him to get what he wanted.

The pleasure took her breath away.

She closed her eyes and opened them again, seeing the stars winking between the branches of the rose briar he had built around them.

Here was a man big enough to take anything he wanted - a fae king with the power to make the natural world bend to his will.

Yet he tended to her as if she were precious.

When he slipped a huge finger inside her, Miranda felt herself begin to fly apart.

"Bron," she whimpered.

He fed on her frantically and she rode on the wings of a pleasure so acute she was afraid she would die.

He groaned against her as he teased out every last twinge of ecstasy.

Then he crawled up beside her and pulled her into his arms.

"Bron," she moaned again, as if she had forgotten every other word in the English language.

"Good girl," he murmured. "Sleep now."

"I need you," she managed to whisper back.

"You want me," he chuckled. "For which I am grateful. But what you need now is rest, mortal. When you wake, we can talk about the rings around our fingers."

She wanted to protest, she really did.

But once again, he seemed to read her mind, sliding his rough fingers through her hair so gently in just the perfect way to make it impossible for her to stay awake.

13

———

MIRANDA

Miranda woke the next morning awash in happiness.

Bron's strong arms were still around her, and the scent of the garden at dawn was incredible - fragrant roses and a dewy earthiness that filled her senses.

She stretched and Bron stretched, too.

"Good morning, lass," he murmured into her hair, sending shivers down her spine.

"Good morning," she whispered back.

He twined his hand with hers and she looked down to the see the inky vines twisting around their ring fingers.

A thousand worries crowded in the background, but at the front of her mind there was only joy and wonder.

She had always been too wrapped up in work to do much dating. She'd thought it would take a miracle for her to find the time to get to know a guy.

Now she was apparently going tattoo-steady with a massive hunky king.

And he seemed like he was *very* pleased about it.

The tattoos were only around their fingers though, they

didn't cover up to their wrists like the ones the others shared.

"Ready for a swim?" he asked.

She laughed. "Really?"

"Sure," he said. "The creek is right down the hill. We can get in a quick swim before we meet the others."

"I just have to get my stuff from the car first," Miranda said.

Bron lifted his hand away from hers and their little den opened up, vines unfurling and pulling away.

She pulled on her swimsuit again first, realizing it wouldn't look good for her to be caught buck naked in the garden. Then they walked together to her car, where Miranda grabbed her purse and shopping bag from yesterday, glad that she had a cosmetic bag and fresh clothing so that she could clean herself up a little.

And so that the others wouldn't know she'd slept over with Bron.

But I have a tattoo on my finger.

She sighed.

That ship had sailed. A tattoo on the hand didn't leave a lot of room for a relationship to start off in privacy. So much for keeping things quiet.

But the more she thought about it, the more she realized that she wasn't sure she wanted to keep things quiet.

She had some things to figure out, but she felt peaceful in a way she never had before. That had to count for something.

"Race you to the creek," Bron offered, his eyes twinkling.

She laughed and took off without agreeing. She needed every advantage in a race against a guy with legs as long as his.

He must have been holding back because she reached the bank long before he did.

"Nice," he said, looking her appreciatively up and down.

Sheesh, she'd probably been jiggling all over the place tearing downhill in her suit. Somehow, she kept forgetting to be self-conscious around the burly king.

She grinned back at him and he offered her his hand to help her into the water.

Once in, she removed her suit and washed it with her mini-hand sanitizer as Bron looked on, bemused.

Then she washed her body as he watched with a heated expression.

"Can I wash you too?" she offered shyly.

But he shook his head.

"Oh," she said, feeling stupid.

Had she misunderstood what happened between them?

"You see those vines around your finger?" he asked her, as if reading her thoughts.

She nodded.

"Do you know what they mean?"

"Sort of," she said.

"I want you to understand completely before they grow up over your hand and around your wrist," he said gruffly.

"So tell me," she said.

"Get dressed and I will," he said.

He stepped into the water, submerging and then coming up and shaking himself like her parents' old Labrador used to do after a bath.

She managed not to laugh.

"Go on, go," he said. "Or I'll lose my resolve."

She climbed out and decided to air dry for a minute or two before getting dressed.

"Gods, woman," he growled from the water.

"What's the story with the tattoo?" she asked primly.

"You are my queen," he said simply. "When we seal that bond by fully consummating our union, the vines will crawl around our hands and we will spend the rest of your life-time together."

Miranda opened her mouth and closed it again.

That's why he didn't want to do anything more last night. He was giving her one last chance to back out.

"That's the short explanation," he said.

"I appreciate knowing the unvarnished truth," she told him. "So basically our relationship is permanent when that happens? No matter what?"

"If you have any doubts about ruling the Wilds," he told her, "now is the time to head for the hills."

"We're already in the hills," she teased.

"Well, time to head for the city then," he told her. "But I can't promise I won't follow and try to bring you home."

"Home," she said, testing out the word.

Twenty-four hours ago she would never have used that word to describe the woods, or anywhere without a walk-in closet.

But now, somehow it felt just right.

Except for that fragment of mirror. Her mind kept going back to it. She tried to push the thought away, but there was no way to get around it. It was all tied together somehow.

She began getting dressed so as to give herself a little space to think.

If her boss had been somehow involved with evil fae, this might be messy. Maybe even so messy that Bron wouldn't want her anymore.

But she had to give Mr. Ward a chance to explain himself. She owed him that much.

"Everything okay?" Bron asked.

"Yes, sure," she said. "Just thinking about work stuff. I don't usually take this much time off."

"You were attending to your missives after midnight last night," he laughed.

"Being an executive assistant is kind of a twenty-four seven job," she replied, trying to smile.

"Do you like your work?" he asked.

"Most of the time," she told him honestly.

"You will miss it when you are queen," he said sadly.

She hadn't thought about that.

"I'm not queen yet," she told him. "I'm just going to run and check my messages. Meet me at the car when you're done."

He nodded.

She took one last look at his huge, gorgeous body, glistening in the early morning sunlight.

Then she turned and hightailed it for the car, hoping Mr. Ward had emailed her back.

There had to be a way to get to the bottom of it all with some reasonable explanation.

14

———

BRON

Bron was just getting dressed when he heard Miranda scream his name.

He bolted up the hill to find her, terrified that whatever had been occupying that last shard of glass had found her.

How could you allow her to roam about alone?

He should have followed her, protected her. It was his duty.

She was his rightful queen. He knew that, even if she did not.

When he reached the garden, he spotted her in the driveway.

But she was not alone. There were so many vehicles that her car was nearly blocked in. People were pouring out of them, wearing work gear and carrying strange equipment.

"What's happening?" he asked her.

"They're here to tear down the trees," she moaned. "This wasn't supposed to happen yet. I just texted Sara and Tabitha. What are we supposed to do?"

There was no time to ponder her words. One of the

workers had already climbed a nearby tree using some kind of harness. They watched in horror as he began removing branches and tossing them down to his partners below.

Bron felt the tree's pain as if his own limbs were being rent from his body. He fought the urge to lash out in defense and tried to use his words instead, for Miranda's sake. He didn't want her to see the things he wanted to do to the attackers.

"*Who's in charge here?*" he boomed.

Everyone stopped what they were doing and turned to him.

"I am," a man said, striding forward. "And you're trespassing on private property."

"I'm the executive assistant to the man who owns all of this," Miranda piped up. "And I'm here on his orders. Where's Larry?"

"Bullshit," the foreman said. "I don't know who Larry is, but the boss's orders are to tear this place to the ground. Today. I'm calling the cops."

"He doesn't even own this land yet," Miranda pointed out.

"I can't get involved in an argument about real estate," the foreman said. "I was hired to do a job and if you two don't get the hell out of the way, I'll have police involved."

"We already have police involved," Miranda said, smiling down at her phone.

"What the hell?" the man stammered, then headed off to talk with the workers.

"I know what I need to do, Bron," Miranda said softly. "I'm going to go talk to my boss, face to face. I'm going to convince him that what he's doing here is wrong. Will you be okay until the others get here?"

I can't let her go alone.

I can't let them destroy this forest.

"Let's wait for them together," he offered. "Then we can both go talk to your boss."

As much as it pained him to leave the forest, his instinct to protect his queen trumped everything else.

"No, that's not a good idea," Miranda said, looking startled. "He's not fond of strangers and I'll have a hard enough time convincing him on my own. Please just take care of this. I'll report back soon."

"Oh," Bron said stupidly. "Sure, I'll stay. But, Miranda..."

He wanted to tell her what he felt for her, to explain how much she meant to him, but he didn't have the words.

"Yes?" she asked, looking impatient.

"Be careful," he told her.

"Sure, of course," she said, smiling up at him with those beautiful sparkly eyes.

She ran to her car and pulled out of the driveway, weaving between the vehicles that had brought the workers.

Bron felt as if his heart were being pulled into pieces before she even left his sight.

How would he bear it as she drove farther away from him and his realm?

15

MIRANDA

Miranda tried to keep her eyes on the road, but it was hard not to keep staring at the vines around her ring finger.

Her whole world felt unfamiliar, yet filled with hope. The shaded ridge above the road was a deeper, more beautiful green, the terra cotta roof of the cottages a rich pumpkin, the air a little sweeter.

And Miranda herself felt unstoppable.

She had friends. She had a boyfriend - no, a *king*.

And she was going to convince Cullen Ward to call off his pet project, one way or the other.

Her plan was to try her best to convince him just by laying out the facts. He was a smart man. She hoped he would see the error of his ways. If not...

Though she hated to do it, she would use her powers if she had to. This was for the greater good.

The weird thing was, she wasn't sure if they would work on him.

The more she thought about it, the more she suspected

Mr. Ward was actually aware of her power. He often encouraged her to *convince* people to do things.

She had never been sure if he thought there was anything special about her, or if he just thought she was charismatic and good with people.

But now that she knew more about herself, it all started to make a lot more sense. Why else had such a powerful man been so eager to hire her at such a young age, especially when she had almost no resumé at all compared to his other choices?

Her phone rang on the car speaker and she pressed the button to pick up.

"Miranda Cannon," she said automatically.

"Miranda." Cullen Ward's voice was low and smooth with a slight rumble. "You wanted to speak with me."

"Thank you so much for calling me back, sir," she said. "Are you back in the office? I'm headed there now, and I was hoping we could sit down together—"

"—I'm leaving the office now on a business matter," he said brusquely.

"Oh," Miranda said.

"We can set something up for next week if you want," Mr. Ward offered. "Or you can get to the point."

Crap.

"Mr. Ward, you may not know this, but I'm originally from Tarker's Hollow," she said.

"Of course I knew that," he chuckled. "Why do you think I sent you to that silly party?"

"I see," she said. "I know you have your reasons for choosing the Rosethorn Valley site, but I've been doing some research, and I think there are two better options in Maryland, where you'll also have a tax advantage. The people in Rosethorn Valley, they—"

"—I'm going to cut you off right there, Miranda," Mr. Ward said. "This is not a conversation I'm going to have with my assistant. I've made up my mind about the site and that's all you need to know. I've told you what I want, now it's your job to make it happen. Do I make myself clear?"

His voice had grown cold and sharp.

"Yes, sir," she said, setting her jaw.

"Excellent," he replied, his voice smooth and modulated once more. "I'll see you at the office on Monday."

He hung up without saying good-bye.

"*Shit*," she said to herself, slamming her palm on the steering wheel. "*Shit, shit, shit.*"

After all the years she'd worked for him, he still wouldn't let her finish a sentence.

Now she would have to turn the car back around and tell her new friends that she had failed before she had even had a chance to try.

But somehow, she just couldn't bring herself to pull over.

Her hands stayed on the wheel and her foot stayed on the gas, and she found herself pulling onto I-95, and heading straight for the city.

Another idea was beginning to occur to her.

It was a crazy plan, maybe even an idiotic plan.

But it was the only plan she had, and she was the only one who could possibly pull it off.

16

BRON

Bron stood in the driveway, glaring at the industrious workers as he inwardly agonized about his queen.

Tabitha's car pulled up a few minutes later.

Tabitha, Tristan, Sara, and Dorian hopped out.

"Miranda just left a little while ago," he told Sara. "Can you call her? Tell her to come back for me."

"Sure, but where is she going?" Sara asked instead of just calling.

"Please, just call her," he asked again, more urgently.

Kings did not beg favors from mortals, but he didn't know what else to do.

She slipped the communication device out of her pocket and began tapping its glassy surface immediately.

Lights flashed in the trees and for a moment he thought it was some trick of Tristan's.

But the colorful lights were atop a car.

"The police are here," Tabitha said, sounding relieved as she jogged over to meet them.

The foreman of the work crew headed for the police car

as well. If he was going up against Tabitha, Bron almost felt sorry for him.

"I can't seem to reach her," Sara said turning back to Bron. "I'm texting her though, so if she sees it maybe she'll come back. Did you guys have an argument or something?"

"No," he said. "Gods, no. She's going to ask her boss to stop all of this. But I don't want her alone when there's still something out there. We don't know what kind of foul creature that last shard housed."

Sara observed him with sympathetic eyes. "You care about her."

He held up his hand so she could see the vines running around his finger.

"Oh," she said, trying not to smile.

"You can smile," he told her. "I'm happy too. Except that I can't stand being away from her."

"Philadelphia is half an hour away," Sara told him. "She'll be back really soon. And then hopefully, we can celebrate."

They looked over to where Tabitha was pointing at the trees.

The police officer was shaking his head.

"Come on," the foreman yelled angrily to his crew. "Pack it up."

Tabitha had been successful, for now.

"We'll stick around to make sure they really leave," Sara said.

Bron nodded, feeling Miranda's absence more keenly than ever now that the land was out of danger and his focus was no longer split.

"*Ask forgiveness, not permission,*" Tabitha said indignantly heading their way with Tristan and Dorian in tow. "What is this world coming to?"

"Is that what they said they were doing?" Sara asked. "Thank God Bron and Miranda were here to catch them."

"Thank God for someone like Dale Evans being on the Tarker's Hollow police force," Tabitha said, shaking her head. "I'm glad he ran them off, but I have a feeling we're going to have to keep a sharp eye on this place."

"What were you doing here so early, brother?" Dorian asked.

Bron blinked.

"I have an idea," Tristan said, looking at Bron's hand.

"Ah," Dorian said with a big smile. "I see congratulations are in order. Where's the lucky lass?"

"She went to Philadelphia to talk to her boss," Sara said quietly. "If she succeeds, then he'll stop all this. And we all know how persuasive Miranda can be."

"Genius," Dorian said. "Well played, brother."

"It's not a *game*, Dorian. I didn't *play* it," Bron exploded. "I love her and she's out there without me, with a piece still missing from the mirror, and gods know what's still on the loose."

"My apologies, brother," Dorian said. "That's not what I meant. But I am certain she's fine."

"How can you say that she's fine?" Bron demanded. "You've seen what's out there. You've seen that it takes all of us to fight it."

"The creatures from that mirror could have gone far and wide," Dorian replied. "But we found every single one of them right here in Rosethorn Valley."

"We should be more concerned that the rest of us might have to face whatever it is without Miranda," Tristan said lightly.

The compliment to his queen's power and bravery mollified Bron slightly and he sighed in resignation.

"Let us wait for her in the garden, brother," Dorian suggested. "We will be more comfortable there."

Bron allowed himself to be led off the driveway and into the soothing greens and cheerful colors of the rose garden. It was hard not to think of his night spent there with his queen, but he did his best to push the thoughts aside for now.

Miranda would be back very soon, surely his brothers were correct. And then they would face the next challenge together.

17

MIRANDA

Miranda parked the car in her reserved space and slipped out into the underground parking lot. She tried giving herself a pep talk as she approached the elevator.

"You can do this, Miranda," she muttered, as if maybe saying the words out loud might make them true. "You did it the other day without even trying."

Her powers had never been so strong before. It must have something to do with Bron, and their connection.

Too bad he wasn't with her now. The distance between them was like a tangible thing - an elastic band stretched way too thin. But just the thought of him gave her courage.

She pressed the button for the elevator and hoped it would be empty. The doors slid open and one of the other executives' assistants slipped out.

"Oh, hey, Miranda," the fastidiously dressed older woman said, eyes wide. "Don't you look... casual?"

"I'm off today," Miranda said. "Just grabbing something from my desk."

"Don't let Ward see you like that," the assistant said over her shoulder as she headed to her car.

"That's the plan," Miranda said to herself as the doors slid shut.

She pressed the button for the top floor and closed her eyes, trying to conjure her best mental image of her boss.

"I am a carbon copy of Cullen Ward," she told herself. "I look exactly like him."

She felt a sort of whisper all around her and when she opened her eyes she almost jumped.

Cullen Ward's reflection stared back at her from the mirrored wall of the elevator. He was looking crisp, freshly shaven, wearing a bespoke suit - exactly as she had pictured him.

"Okay," she whispered to herself.

Even her whisper was a deep bass.

The doors slid open.

"Mr. Ward," someone said in surprise. "You're back."

She turned to see one of her least favorite colleagues, Frank Espen, blinking at her in abject horror.

Espen's tie was loosened and his sleeves were rolled up. His required suit jacket was nowhere to be seen. He clearly hadn't expected to see his boss again today.

"Pull yourself together, Espen," she snapped, mustering what she hoped was an appropriate level of confidence. "I hope you don't get undressed every time I leave the building."

"N-n-no, sir," Espen stammered as he rolled his sleeves down.

She turned on her heel and headed for Ward's office, trying not to skip for joy.

It worked. Her magic worked.

Now she just had to get what she had come for and get out again before Ward came back or her power faded.

Anthony, the security guard who protected Mr. Ward's office suite, saluted her as she approached the door.

"Mr. Ward," Anthony said with a polite smile. "Good to see you back so soon."

She nodded at him approvingly, knowing her boss would never spare a kind word for the guard, even though Anthony had been loyal and cheerful for as long as Miranda had worked there.

She placed her hand against the door sensor, praying that the machine would pick up what she was showing it, and not what she actually was. She had no idea if her power extended to machines or not.

If not, this was about to be a very short mission.

For a long moment nothing happened. Did it usually take this long to scan Mr. Ward's hand? After an agonizing few more seconds, the light over the sensor blinked green and the door swung open.

Miranda sighed inwardly, trying to keep her cool outer composure intact. Cullen Ward was supposed to be unflappable.

She stepped inside and waited for the door to click shut behind her before continuing into the suite.

A huge wall of windows looked out over the Philadelphia skyline, but Miranda didn't spare a glance. Instead, she headed straight for the coat closet.

She opened the door and pressed a hidden button inside, then stepped back.

The whole closet interior slid forward and out, revealing that it was basically a small wardrobe tucked inside a much deeper space.

Miranda slipped into the area behind the wardrobe.

I am Cullen Ward. I am Cullen Ward.

She realized almost too late that she wasn't tall enough for the optic scanner that had just flashed to life.

She reached back into the coat closet and grabbed one of Mr. Ward's travel cases, getting it into place and stepping up onto it just in time for the optic scanner to finish warming up.

"I am Cullen Ward," she muttered as the light panned down her face.

A section of wall slid away to reveal a metal box.

She held her breath and thumbed open the latch.

18

BRON

Bron heard the car pulling up and ran for the driveway, the others trailing behind him.

She's back, thank the gods...

But instead of Miranda's car, he saw a sleek silver thing slide into a spot next to the house, between the abandoned work vehicles.

A door opened upward, like a bird trying to clean the feathers under its wing.

A familiar figure stepped out and surveyed the mansion.

Bron staggered backward, unable to believe his eyes.

"Oh my God," Sara whispered loudly. "That's Cullen Ward,"

"This is insane," Tabitha murmured. "What is he doing here?"

"That's not who you think it is," Tristan said.

"You think I don't know one of the top businessmen on the East Coast?" Tabitha said. "He's the man behind all of this. He's on the cover of *Philly Business* this month. Of course that's Cullen Ward."

"No," Bron said, regaining his composure. "That is our brother."

The King of Order strode toward them, sleek and resplendent as the car he had driven up in. The breeze didn't disturb his hair, dust from the gravel lot didn't scuff his polished leather shoes, and his sunglasses shone as if they had never been touched.

"What have we here?" he asked, his deep voice amused.

No one answered.

"What are you doing here, Cullen?" Bron demanded.

"I own this place," the fae king said coldly. "What are *you* doing here?"

"You don't own it yet," Sara retorted.

For a moment Bron was afraid for her. His brother had a temper, and he was known to be cruel, even by fae standards.

But the King of Order merely laughed.

"A detail that will soon be ironed out," Cullen told her with a smile that showed too many perfect teeth.

Sara recoiled.

"So *you* bought this place?" Bron demanded. "*You* wanted to destroy the door between our realms?"

"This place is cursed," Cullen spat.

"How long have you been free in this world?" Dorian asked.

"Long enough to know this realm is better off without the three of you in it," Cullen said. "And better still without the rest of Faerie. I'm going to tear down the veil and close the door between worlds forever. So if you want to go home again, now is the time."

"You first," Bron said with so much hate that he almost didn't recognize his own voice.

"Oh, look at you, brothers, with vines of bonding around

your hands," Cullen remarked, ignoring Bron's challenge. "How adorable. But where is your lucky girl, Bron?"

Miranda.

It hit him suddenly that this was her employer.

This was the man she worked for, the one she was loyal to.

He was the one she had run to today.

Jealousy rose up in him like a viper, filled with poison and inchoate fury.

Each brother had one that stood in opposition. Yet while Dorian and Tristan complemented each other as dark and light, Cullen and Bron were ever at odds.

It didn't help that their parents had always preferred Cullen's exacting nature to Bron's warmth and compassion.

"She didn't stick around, eh, little brother?" Cullen said with a bitter laugh. "Sounds about right."

He hadn't forgotten his brother's cruelty, but he also hadn't been prepared to be the target of it.

Bron lowered his head, ready to charge.

He felt Dorian's steadying hand on his shoulder and held his ground.

For now.

"She's coming right back," Dorian said. "And I hate to break it to you, Cullen, but you won't be tearing anything down. We had your workers sent away."

"Oh, you did?" Cullen asked lightly.

He raised his arm, showing off the lines of his impeccably tailored suit of clothing. He had always been the vain one.

A rumbling sound arose from all around them.

All the work machinery in the drive was turning on. A neat trick, but even Cullen couldn't pilot all these contraptions on his own.

As if in response to his doubts, figures began to emerge from the trees. Each one was fairly humanoid, but seemed to be made entirely of shadow. Bron had never seen his brother do anything like that before. He watched as the shadow fae slid onto the equipment, taking the place of the missing workers.

"No," Bron moaned.

The King of Order watched, an expression of unforgivable satisfaction on his face, as one of the machines lurched forward and plowed into a tree.

Pain ripped through Bron and he bellowed out his misery as he ran to the machine.

Cullen inhaled deeply, as if he were savoring Bron's pain.

Tristan came forward, miniature suns pulsing in each of his hands.

Bron wrapped his arms around the shadowy fae in the machine and tried to pull it from its seat.

It slipped his grasp, easily reshaping itself to avoid him.

Tristan flung a ball of light at the thing and it let out a high-pitched shriek before exploding into nothing.

"Yes, brother," Bron exclaimed.

Together they turned to face their next foe.

But it was more than just the machines now. The whole forest seemed to be filled with shadow fae, belligerently attacking the trees.

19

MIRANDA

iranda gazed down at the tiny shard of mirror, willing it not to be as she recalled it.

But it was. Of course.

There was no doubt that this was the missing glass from the mirror at the mansion.

Which meant that Cullen Ward, one of the most famous businessmen in America, was also involved with the release of evil fae.

She snatched it out of the box before she could chicken out, resisting the impulse to examine the other items.

As fast as she could, she pressed the button to replace the closet and close the door.

She checked the wall mirror on the way back to the suite entry door, and then did a double-take.

The effect of her magic was fading.

She could see Cullen Ward, but she could also see herself beneath him, as if his image had merely been projected onto her, and now the projector was dimming.

"*No*," she moaned, closing her eyes to focus.

Her voice was notably higher. It wasn't quite her own yet, but it was obvious that the disguise was disintegrating.

"Mr. Ward, are you okay in there?" Anthony called from outside the door.

She pictured her boss, willing herself to look and sound like him.

I am Cullen Ward.

"I'm fine, Anthony," she called back to him, relieved to hear her voice was deep again. "But I could use your help."

She needed to get him away from his post, so he wouldn't see her leaving.

"Of course, sir," Anthony replied. "May I come in?"

"No," she said quickly. "I need you to go get me a triple espresso."

"I can ask one of the girls to do that," Anthony offered.

"I want you to do it," she told him quickly.

"But... but that would mean your suite is unguarded," Anthony said nervously. "That's in direct violation of my duties."

"I'm here, aren't I?" she asked, in what she hoped was a frighteningly thunderous voice. "Do you think I can't guard my own office for five minutes?"

"Oh, yes. I mean, of course you can," Anthony said. "I'll go now."

She forced herself to count to twenty before heading to the door.

She placed her palm on the sensor.

It didn't open.

I'm trapped. I'm trapped in his suite.

What kind of person installs security measures to get out of his own office?

Cullen Ward did. Of course he did. He never made anything easy.

She took a breath and tried to focus, but truth of her ability was beginning to dawn on her.

Her magic was stronger because of Bron, that much was true. But it seemed like it was strongest when she was physically close to him.

The more time and distance between them, the more her abilities began to weaken.

Bron, I need you...

She tried to pull up an image of Bron in her mind - huge, muscular, long, messy hair falling around his shoulder, twinkly eyes.

Her heart swelled.

The sensor dinged under her hand.

She dashed into the hallway as fast as she could and hightailed it for the elevator.

"Mr. Ward, are you okay?" Espen called out slavishly.

"Fine," she said in a perfect staccato impression of her impatient boss.

The elevator doors slid shut, and at last she let the illusion fall away from herself and leaned against the back wall, exhausted.

She'd done it.

She just had to get back to Bron and the others with the shard, and everything would be okay.

20

BRON

Bron closed his eyes and called on his gift.

Tristan battled the shadows bravely, but even his light was slowly fading.

Dorian's midnight did no damage to these creatures, they almost seemed to feed on it.

Sara's song had dried up in her throat.

Tabitha stood before the trees the monsters had rent, placing her hands on the suffering bark, trying to heal what had been broken.

They were giving it everything they had, and coming up short.

Somehow, Cullen seemed to draw strength from all their suffering, expanding his army with each fresh agony, as if he were not the King of Order, but the King of Pain.

Don't look at him, Bron told himself, as he had many times as a little boy.

But it was hard not to look at Cullen. He had always drawn the spotlight to himself, seemingly without effort.

Bron reached deep within himself and called to the very roots beneath his feet, and to the branches above.

Rise, my brothers, he said to the trees. *If I cannot protect you, you must fight for yourselves.*

There was a groaning in the forest as roots tore themselves free from the loamy soil and trunks moved out of the path of the equipment.

"Whoa," he heard Sara breathe behind him.

A giant oak wrenched itself from the ground and slammed a massive branch down on a backhoe, which crumpled, smashing its shadowy rider into a fine mist.

A shadow fae driving a bulldozer realized what was going on and tried to turn away from the copper beech tree it was attempting to topple. But the clever beech shivered and bent in the middle, stabbing the bulldozer with dozens of sharp branches.

Bron felt the magic blasting out of his body, as if the forest were sucking it in as hard as he was pushing it out. It wanted to survive. It wasn't ready to go down without a fight.

He pushed a surge of energy out of himself, feeding the trees until the earth seemed to rumble beneath his feet.

Somewhere in the back of his mind, he knew he had never pushed himself this way before.

But none of it mattered.

Miranda was coming back. He was sure of it. He couldn't allow his queen to return to this kind of danger.

As soon as his brother realized what she meant to Bron, he would break her.

And Bron couldn't bear that.

He pushed even harder, drawing on reserves of strength he never knew he had.

But when he opened his eyes, he could see his strength was slipping.

A dump truck plowed through a stand of saplings and hit a big maple so hard it nearly doubled over.

Tristan moved to help, but the light in his hands was smaller now, more like a sunset than a midday blaze.

They were fading, all of them.

How had Cullen amassed such power?

A familiar tug at some deep part of him made Bron wheel around. In the noise of the battle, he must have missed the sound of a car's engine approaching.

Miranda stood at the head of the driveway, clutching something in her hand and looking out over the trees in horror.

21

MIRANDA

Miranda could see that something strange was happening as soon as she pulled into the drive. The trees were thrashing, and darkness hung over the woods like a raging storm, though she had driven through nothing but blue skies and sunshine for the last half an hour.

She parked and dashed out of the car, taking the steps down to the rose garden two at a time, where an unbelievable, horrific scene unfolded before her eyes.

Sara, Dorian, Tristan, and Tabitha stood shoulder to shoulder, launching small balls of light at something that writhed and shivered like a shadow in the trees.

Bron stood before them, his big arms stretched to the heavens, muscles trembling with effort.

His brow was furrowed and sweat poured down his chest.

All around him, the trees were uprooting themselves as if he were lifting them from the ground himself.

She had never seen anyone make an effort like this. It

didn't look like he could keep it up much longer. What would happen when he had nothing left to give?

"*Bron*," she screamed.

His eyes met hers for one agonizing second.

And then she noticed something familiar, but out of place.

"Miranda Cannon," Cullen Ward said smoothly, turning to her from where he stood.

"M-Mr. Ward?" she stammered.

"Are you involved in this in some way?" he asked politely.

He glanced at her hand and his eyes widened slightly.

"*You're* the consort to the King of the Wilds?" he chuckled, recovering. "Oh, Miranda, how could you stoop so low?"

"She's not my consort," Bron roared with strength Miranda didn't think he could spare. "She is my queen."

"Not yet she's not, brother," Ward said coolly. "I only see a ring, a promise of what could be. Perhaps what *will* be. *If* you agree to take her through the veil along with Tristan and Dorian, and then let me destroy the doorway with you on the other side."

"Her life is here," Bron gasped. "And this world deserves our protection."

"Suit yourself," Mr. Ward said.

Miranda had heard that tone from him many times - usually in the boardroom, just before Cullen Ward ruined a company or a career.

"*No*," she cried, running past her boss to join her friends.

When she reached Sara, Miranda held out the mirror shard where the friends could see it, but Cullen Ward could not.

"Oh my God," Sara whispered. "It's him, isn't it?"

"It's him," Miranda confirmed. "Sing to him. Let's put him back where he belongs."

Dorian groaned and pulled a cloak of midnight tightly around Mr. Ward.

"Saint's plaything, Dorian," Ward laughed. "You think I'm afraid of the dark?"

Sara's voice rang out in answer, tired, but clear.

"*SNEAKING OUT of mirror's hold*
You were cruel and you were bold
Stripping Earth of mortal wealth
Without a thought for mortal health
No care for any human kind
Out of fae, out of your mind"

"No," Ward moaned, as soon as he realized what was happening to him. His clothing was whipping in an invisible wind that seemed to draw him toward the mirror fragment.

"*IN THE BUSINESS world you could be tough*
But soon money was not enough
You found you had a taste for pain
Not just for economic gain"

CULLEN WARD SLID TOWARD THEM, his fancy leather shoes carrying him across the wet grass like ice-skates. But he clenched his fists and jaw at the last second and managed to summon enough power to halt himself.

The light in Tristan's hands was almost gone.

Sara's voice grew faint, barely a whisper.

"*Surrender*," Miranda cried. But it came out sounding more like a plea than a command.

Bron met her eyes and the look of sadness in them nearly broke her heart. His lips mouthed the words, *I love you*, before he closed his eyes and placed his palms on the ground.

Miranda watching in horror as the forest all around them drained of color. Trees went gray and then black before collapsing into cold ash, the grass curled up as if burning from invisible flames, birds dropped from the sky as black smoke billowed overhead.

Bron's muscles rippled and strained, like he was attempting to lift the Earth itself. A groan of pain escaped him, the sheer anguish of it chilling Miranda to her core.

"What's happening to him?" Miranda asked, knowing that she didn't really want an answer.

"Bron gets his power from the living world," Tristan explained, the light in his hands growing brighter by the second. "And right now, he is calling on all of it to bolster us."

Bron was consuming the very life of the forest to summon the strength to defeat his brother.

And it was working.

Cullen Ward shuddered but could not move.

Dorian drew a fresh cloak of inky midnight closely around him.

Sara ran forward, mirror outstretched, her voice strong and true.

"Go BACK *into the mirror's hold*
Back into the faerie fold

Where your cruel ways are understood,
And leave this mortal world to Good."

BRON COLLAPSED like a ragdoll from the effort of burning up the life force of the forest to harness its energy.

Miranda felt the last surge of his power flow through her.

"Surrender," she shouted, and Cullen could not help but obey.

He floated toward Sara. Just before he reached her, he looked into the mirror and his features shifted from anger to what Miranda swore was happiness. He let go completely and shrank into a living shadow that was sucked into the mirror shard with an audible pop.

There was a moment of stunned silence.

Then the friends began to cheer. Tristan lifted Tabitha and spun her around in his arms.

Only Miranda seemed to notice that one voice was missing from the chorus.

She ventured to where Bron had knelt a moment ago, but there was no sign he had ever been there.

"Bron," she screamed into the ashen remains of the forest.

But without living trees, she could see a hundred yards in every direction.

And Bron was nowhere to be found.

"Oh, gods," she heard Dorian murmur.

"Miranda," Sara said softly, placing her hands on her shoulders.

"*Bron,*" Miranda screamed again, unable to help herself.

But there was only silence. Not even the birds cried back to her.

They searched the scarred trees, but Miranda's wild king seemed to have disappeared as if he had never existed at all.

It's my fault. If my power to compel were greater, he wouldn't have had to sacrifice himself...

Sirens in the distance roused her from the wreckage of her mind.

"They're coming because of the smoke," Tabitha cried. "We have to put the mirror back together before they get here."

Miranda stood, frozen in place, unwilling to stop the search.

"We'll find him soon," Sara said comfortingly. "But we can't have let all this happen in vain."

Miranda allowed herself to be led into the mansion.

She watched as her friends placed the last shard.

Tabitha approached the glass, pressed both palms to it and closed her eyes.

For a moment it felt as if all the air had been sucked out of the room. Then the surface of the mirror stopped showing a reflection. The glass swirled like water.

Miranda saw the fachan, the kelpie, the will o' the wisps, and other monsters she didn't recognize. She saw Cullen Ward, still smiling as he fell deeper and deeper into the mirror.

Desperately, she searched for Bron. What if he had been sucked into the mirror somehow? Would she ever find him again?

But if he was in the mirror, she did not see him.

Light emanated from Tristan's whole body and Dorian pulled inky midnight around the mirror itself.

There was a sound like a gong and Miranda realized it was the grandfather clock in the foyer. It struck the hour over and over.

Surely, she miscounted, because she swore it counted out thirteen hours.

"You are whole again," Miranda whispered.

Then the room suddenly went quiet.

Dorian lifted midnight, Tristan extinguished his light.

And the five of them were standing in front of a beautiful antique mirror. There wasn't a crack on it. It was perfectly lovely, and perfectly normal.

"We have to go," Tabitha said.

They all ran for their cars.

Miranda pulled down the driveway alone and headed for Tarker's Hollow. She didn't particularly want to go to the Inn, but she wasn't sure where else she could go.

She was truly alone.

Her whole body felt hollowed out and empty.

Bron...

Her phone rang and she answered with the car speaker.

"Miranda Cannon," she said automatically.

"You're coming to my place," Tabitha said firmly. "We've got about a hundred spare bedrooms and you're not leaving Rosethorn Valley until we find Bron."

"Thank you," Miranda said softly, trying not to cry. "Thank you so much."

"That's what friends are for," Tabitha said gruffly. "Now get over here. We've got to figure out what happened to your guy."

"I'm on my way," Miranda said, smiling through her tears.

22

MIRANDA - LATER

Ten months after that fateful day, Miranda stood in the circle of forest that had been invisibly burned down in the deadly battle with the notorious fae king who used to be her boss.

So much had happened since, but if she closed her eyes, she could still see Bron as clear as day, kneeling on the blackened ground, burning his beloved forest, the source of his power, to save her realm.

Miranda and her friends had done all they could to find him, exhausting both magic and mortal methods. But there was no trace of the King of the Wilds.

But Miranda hadn't given up. She never would.

Nothing just disappears...

She surveyed the land with grim satisfaction.

Cullen Ward had surprised her one more time.

When the board decided he had been missing long enough they unsealed his living directive.

Everyone at Dolor Enterprises was shocked to find that Cullen Ward had left his empire in the hands of his executive assistant, Miranda Cannon.

It had been up to Miranda to oversee all operations at Dolor as well as to allocate and maintain his assets.

The first thing she had done was to stop the development of the lab in Rosethorn Valley.

"Mr. Ward had a vision for this project that he never shared with us," she had lied to the board. "To try to continue would be irresponsible."

Somehow, she had no problem convincing them.

But she had seen Ward's notes, scrawled in the leatherbound journal in his safe.

The one-time King of Order had learned that pain increased his powers.

He'd posed as one of Dorian's fae creatures, in order to get him in enough trouble to be imprisoned in the midnight loop, but not before he'd made a deal, securing his own release from the mirror prison.

Once Dorian was taken care of, Tristan and Bron weren't far behind.

With his brothers out of the way, he was free to pursue his own unsavory machinations, and build his empire of pain.

The lab at Rosethorn Valley would have experimented on innocent animals, their suffering giving him an endless power source.

And the psychological pain this knowledge would have caused the residents of the little borough when they learned about the animal experiments would only have added to his strength.

Cullen Ward wanted to own this world.

And then he wanted to destroy it with its own agony.

He had truly become the King of Pain.

This knowledge made it very easy for Miranda to send the bulk of his fortune toward charity.

After all, he had a lot of cruelty to make up for. She was certain he had caused plenty of pain that she would never know about.

Under Miranda's direction, a small fortune had gone to humane shelters across the country. The foundation she formed also gave generously to veterans' funds, elder care, food banks, conservation programs and medical and arts foundations. It gave money to dig wells and educate children in places where books and water were scarce.

And at last, the purchase of the mansion and the land it was built on was finalized, and then it was donated to the Rosethorn Valley Historical Society.

Miranda stopped when it was clear there was enough left in Mr. Ward's funds for him to be wealthy, but not dangerously so, if he ever returned. Enough for her actions to be unusual, but not completely suspicious.

But she knew he was never coming back.

The months of researching and giving had been incredibly rewarding as well as a lot of hard work. Each moment of helping others gave her some small respite from the agony of missing Bron. He loved living things - it would have warmed his heart to know she was doing his work as best she could in his absence.

Miranda knew it was time to move on from the part of her life dictated by Cullen Ward.

But it was impossible to see a future without Bron in it.

She looked over the ruined land.

The historical society had held a huge fundraiser to replant the whole area. Tiny trees dotted the landscape. One day they would grow strong and tall again and flowers would bloom once more.

It was beginning to look a little better already. Months of rain and sunshine were doing their work.

She wrapped her arms around herself, feeling as though she might fly apart with the pain of missing her king.

"Oh, Bron," she whispered. "The only person I've ever really wanted to compel is you. Please. Come back to me."

There was a murmur in the air, and she sensed movement before her.

Miranda's lips parted in wonder as she saw tender shoots of grass poking up from the muddy ground.

The little trees burst with leaves before her eyes, and the foliage surrounding the scarred land began to blossom with beautiful flowers.

It was as if the earth itself were coming alive around her, springtime moving in fast forward, filling the air with the lush scent of flowers and new life.

She caught a glimpse of a giant stag, leaping among the new growth, then dashing out of sight.

"Bron," she breathed.

She turned, barely daring to hope.

"Miranda," he said, smiling down at her with twinkling eyes.

His big body was naked and perfect. He was so beautiful she couldn't speak.

Instead she fell into his arms, weeping.

"I'm here, my queen," he said into her hair.

"Where did you go?" she sobbed. "Why did you leave me?"

"I would never leave you," he told her. "But I depleted my powers. I had to sleep again."

"You were *hibernating*?" she asked in wonder.

"I guess you could say that," he said. "Life is reborn in the springtime. Though sometimes it gets a little help."

"I compelled you," she said, realizing.

"You compelled me," he agreed. "And I'm glad. I was ready to come home."

"I could have done that at any time," she moaned.

"No," he told her. "It wouldn't have worked until spring, until the wilds were ready to return."

"Please don't ever do that again," she said, relishing the feeling of his strong arms around her, wishing he would never let her go.

"I have no plan to be even an inch away from you, ever again," he declared.

She went up on her toes and pressed kisses to his cheeks and eyelids.

He swept her up in his arms and carried her through the field.

Miranda watched the world spring to life all around them. Every place Bron's feet touched the earth, greenery burst from the ground, spreading outward, covering the hillside in beauty.

At last they reached the creek, where older trees still stretched their branches overhead like a ceiling.

As the blossoms unfurled around them, so did her heart, seeking the radiance of her king.

23

BRON

Bron held Miranda in his arms.

Pleasure surged through his body. He had not only returned to the mortal realm, but he had been renewed - his powers were at their peak.

His heart ached at the sorrow he'd caused her. He'd disappeared without a chance to tell her where he was, or if he would return. Even one cycle of the seasons must have seemed like an eternity.

But he could see by the inky black vines, still dark against her pale finger, that her love for him had not faded.

He placed her gently on the bank.

"I am sorry that I frightened you," he told her solemnly. "I want to know everything that happened while I was sleeping. But first I want to finish what we started the last time we were here."

"I want to be your queen," she replied.

The words washed away the ache in his heart with a wave of pure happiness. He bent to remove her clothing, feeling frantic to make her wish, and his need, a reality.

At last she stood before him, naked and beautiful, her titian hair hanging in loose curls down her back.

He lifted her in his arms again and carried her to the edge of the water where a soft bed of moss awaited.

He closed his eyes and called to the trees, letting his renewed power flow freely.

A whisper of branches told him they were doing his bidding, extending around them to form a beautiful shelter where he could claim his queen.

But he had no eyes for the trees. He saw only Miranda, her bright hair fiery against the green of the moss, her arms extended, urging him close.

He pressed his lips to hers and tasted eternity as her light moan pierced him with desire.

He pulled away to gaze into her eyes. "I will love you forever, Miranda Cannon. Will you be my queen?"

"Yes," she moaned.

He buried his face in her neck, inhaling her delicate scent, memorizing the softness of her skin, the warmth of her pulse.

But he could feel her nipples, stiff like buds against his chest, longing for his touch.

She whimpered as he moved down to lick one into his mouth.

He savored the delicate texture and the melody of her cries as he teased and lavished her nipples with attention.

Miranda tangled her fingers in his hair, driving him wild with the delicious scrape of her nails against his scalp.

He moved lower, pressing kisses against her warm belly as he nudged her thighs apart. He needed to taste her before he claimed her, needed it more than his next breath.

Miranda froze as he pressed his mouth to her tender sex.

He stroked her firmly with his tongue and the sounds

she made were incredible. He lapped at her again and again, teasing her, exploring exactly what made her wiggle and scream with the most despair and delight.

At last he felt her hips trembling with the need for satisfaction.

He crawled up and caged her head in his arms, pressing his forehead to hers.

"I need you, Miranda," he groaned.

"Please," she whispered brokenly.

24

MIRANDA

Miranda was pinned between the soft mossy bank and the exquisite hardness of her king.

Sensation and emotion ripped through her, threatening to unhinge her mind.

"I need you," she whimpered.

"Easy, my love," he crooned.

She felt him take himself in his hand, pressing hot steel against her opening.

He was so large it should have been frightening, but she felt herself melt like butter around him, accepting him slowly and painlessly until at last he was fully seated.

"Miranda." It sounded like a prayer.

"Please," she begged again, as if she had forgotten any other word existed.

Bron began to move, slowly.

She felt the pleasure mounting as if it were unfurling from the ground, tender shoots exploding out of the earth, flying toward the heavens.

She heard her own cries of ecstasy as if from outside of her body.

"Miranda," he groaned again, pounding into her faster, filling her again and again.

Another climax took her and this time she saw flowers blooming behind her eyes.

When he pushed her over the edge for a third time, she swore she heard birds singing a symphony.

Bron cried out his own pleasure and she relished the feeling of his hot seed jetting into her, filling her with his love and renewal.

When they were both sated, he curled himself around her, and they lay there in happy silence, breathing each other in.

"I missed you," she murmured at last.

"I could tell," he teased.

He twined his fingers through hers, and she saw that each of them now had vines extending up their hands and encircling their wrists.

"It's real now," she whispered.

"Are you sorry?" he asked her.

"*No*," she said, horrified. "Are you?"

He laughed and the happy sound of it seemed to reverberate in her blood. "I could never be sorry."

"I could stay here forever," she told him. "But it doesn't feel right not to make sure your brothers know you're home."

"My brothers?" he scoffed.

"*Everyone* has been searching for you for almost a year," she scolded him. "You would think that if you can just go to sleep for months at a time, you might tell your family about it."

"They were really looking for me?" he asked, sounding surprised.

"Look, I don't know what sibling rivalry is like in your

world," she told him. "But it sounds terrifying. In this world, a lot of siblings recover from their rivalries as adults. And they find comfort in their unique shared history."

He looked thoughtful.

"Believe me, Bron, *no one* here will share a history like yours," she told him. "Dorian and Tristan are desperate to find you. They love you."

A smile split his handsome face. "Well, let's go find my brothers then."

She smiled back and wondered if anyone had ever looked forward to such an unusual family reunion: three brothers, three kings and their queens, a triumvirate formed in desperation, tempered by invisible fire, and reborn on a beautiful spring morning, when it seemed that anything was possible.

As the trees spread their branches once more, she saw that the entire hillside of rhododendrons had blossomed around them. The sky was brilliant blue overhead, and the birdsong seemed to carry a deeper meaning.

Like they were celebrating the return of their king.

25

BRON

A few days later, Bron waited in the rose garden outside the mansion, with his brothers by his side.

He felt buttoned up and sweaty in the formal suit of human clothing, but Tristan and Dorian had assured him that Miranda would like it, and he was determined to do all he could to make this day special for her.

He looked at his brothers, each resplendent in his own fine suit, all of them looking as happy as he felt.

Chairs had been set up in the rose garden for friends and family. Bron didn't recognize many of the faces, but Officer Dale Evans and his wife were there, with Helen Thayer and her boyfriend seated beside them. The woman who ran the grocery store, and Carl from Le Sucre had joined them as well.

In time, Bron knew, he would get to know all the people who were important to their circle of friends.

For now, it was enough to be spending his time volunteering with Miranda, Sara, Tabitha, and his brothers to get the mansion back in shape.

With the help of Jack Harkness, a carpenter from Tarker's Hollow, Bron was learning to be an excellent woodworker. "You sure have a way with wood," Jack would say, shaking his head in wonder. Jack didn't realize Bron had a serious advantage with anything that had to do with trees.

They hoped to have the place ready for tours and history lessons in the next year. Miranda and Tabitha were working with the local school district to plan a Rosethorn Valley History summer day camp.

It was good to see Miranda happy. When Bron first met her, she had seemed as buttoned-up as he was laid-back.

Now she laughed easily, and he saw a wild side of her that he hadn't dreamed he would be able to set loose so quickly.

His new friend, Jack, began to play the acoustic guitar softly, which Bron knew was the signal that things were about to begin.

Tristan and Dorian straightened up and their friends in the chairs all turned to look as the freshly polished doors of the mansion swung open.

Sara came out first, her long dark hair swirled in a loose bun and topped with a lace veil. Her gossamer gown trailed behind her as she walked slowly past their friends to stand beside Dorian, whose expression was steely. Bron knew him well enough to know it was because he was trying not to cry.

Tabitha came next, in white satin with a tiny, box-shaped hat over her glossy hair. Tristan smiled and Bron hoped their friends didn't see the slight glow that emanated from his brother's body as he joyfully watched his betrothed arrive at his side.

Bron held his breath as he waited for one more queen to grace the doorway.

Miranda stood in the threshold for just a moment, then time seemed to stand still as she moved toward him.

Her fiery hair fell in loose cascades down her back. She wore a simple cotton dress, her only adornment a circlet of baby's breath in her hair. Her feet were bare. She was just as he loved her best - completely herself.

He felt almost gutted with love.

The mayor of Rosethorn Valley came forward and began to speak the words of the ceremony, but Bron could hardly hear them.

Miranda was beside him, gazing up at him, her eyes hazy with love.

He managed to say his piece when it was his turn and slide a ring onto her finger.

The ring and the ceremony were extraneous, of course, his promise to be her king was older than the custom of rings and saying words by rote. And they had already shared the true ring that would mark their bond forever.

But he wanted to belong to her in every way, to express his love in every ceremony that might carry meaning for her and her kind.

Suddenly, everyone was cheering and he knew it was time for their kiss.

Miranda flung her arms around his neck and he lifted her up and swung her, pressing his lips hungrily to hers.

"Easy, Bron," she giggled after a moment.

"I'm the King of the Wilds," he growled teasingly.

"Yes, but we don't need to *show* them," she teased back.

"You have five minutes to make your excuses," he told her. "Then I'm taking you into the woods to have my way with you, lass."

"Okay," she said. "But I'm going to need more than five minutes. We have a party to throw."

He glanced over to where his brothers and their wives were laughing and greeting their friends. Someone had turned on light-hearted music and it was playing through a set of speakers on the porch. A BBQ grill was going on the lawn in front of the mansion and he could already smell a delightful assortment of charring meats. The smoke curled upward toward a sky that was growing pink with twilight.

"You know what?" he said. "I actually like that idea."

It was incredible to think that there was anything he might like to do that involved other fae and humans. He had spent an eternity trying to make his excuses and get back to the woods.

"Are you getting domesticated on me?" she teased.

"No, I just want cake," he laughed. "But maybe you have tamed me, just a little. I would follow you anywhere, you know that, don't you?"

"I do know that," Miranda told him, her beautiful eyes serious now. "I love you, my king."

"And I love you, my queen," he told her. "I will love you forever."

***

Thanks for reading King of the Wilds!

Are you ready for more steamy fae king action? Do you want to know exactly what Cullen Ward saw on the other side of the veil that made him smile and give up the fight? Do you want to learn about the heartbreak that led him to become the King of Pain, and find out if he can redeem himself when he gets an unexpected second chance?

Then keep reading for a sample of King of Pain, or grab your copy now:

https://www.tashablack.com/kingofpain.html

KING OF PAIN (SAMPLE)

1

CULLEN

Cullen Ward roared and pushed his magic to its limit.

He felt the strain on his mind as well as his muscles as he brought an army of shadows to life around him to hold strong against the light.

A bead of sweat stung his eyes.

All three of his brothers and their queens stood before him, furiously gathering their forces to oust Cullen from the human realm. The King of Light assaulted him with magical bursts while the King of Darkness smothered him in an inky cloak of midnight. The King of the Wilds was burning the very life force from the surrounding forest to bolster their attacks.

Seeing the three of them work together was almost more painful than their magical onslaught.

Almost.

Cullen himself had once been the King of Order, but he had learned to feed on pain, an endless fuel source in this miserable realm.

And yet even with so much power at his fingertips, he

still felt himself inexorably pushed through the veil between the mortal realm and the fae.

How can they stand against me at all? I should be able to demolish them with a thought.

But somehow, his brothers were willing to drain themselves to push him back into Faerie. They were pushing harder than he'd ever imagined they could.

Cullen glanced around at their queens, fighting their own hearts out beside them, and he understood.

His brothers had something to fight for.

It was only a matter of time before they bested him. He could already smell the forest around them burning with the invisible fire of his youngest brother's life essence. The fool was willing to sacrifice himself for these mortals.

As the veil between worlds opened to suck him in, the faintest hint of another scent slipped between realms and caressed his senses.

Cullen froze, all thoughts of the battle forgotten.

Jessica...

The redolence of tea roses and vanilla sent his memory reeling.

He reclines on a soft blanket in the shade of a mighty oak. She sits beside him, legs curled under her, jotting notes in a leather bound journal. The scratch of her pen against the paper tickles his senses.

Suddenly he had no strength left to fight his brothers.

And more importantly, he had no desire to resist.

If any part of Jessica was on the other side, he had no more need of the mortal realm after all.

His brother's invisible fire was expanding now, licking at the stone wall that separated the garden and the mansion from the woods.

Cullen was barely holding on. The power was almost too much for him to resist.

But it also proved too much for his little brother.

The King of the Wilds fell onto his side, the last of his life energy spent. His queen wailed in agony.

Her pain was exquisite. It surged into Cullen, filling him with all the power he could handle - more than enough to defeat his remaining brothers and end the short lives of their mortal queens.

He knew exactly what he needed to do next.

For the first time in decades, a genuine smile graced Cullen Ward's stern features. He took one final look at his brothers.

And then he let go.

2
————

CULLEN

Cullen landed hard on his ass on the checkerboard floor of an empty ballroom.

He knew where he was immediately - his brother Dorian had spent centuries wasting away in this glorified prison.

Cullen had no intention of doing the same.

"Your majesty." A familiar voice floated across the room, cloyingly sweet and groveling.

He turned to see a woman in a bird mask and ball gown approaching, bent practically in half with delight as she bowed and curtseyed her way to him.

"Golda," he said dismissively, recognizing the fae handmaid.

"I see it worked," Golda said. Her voice was soft, but clear as a bell.

"What worked?" he asked.

"I tricked the human girl into breaking the mirror," Golda laughed.

"Why?" he asked.

Had he not sensed Jessica's presence in this place, he

would have murdered Golda where she stood, simply for starting the chain of events that landed him in this wretched place. As it was, he was still undecided about it.

She shrugged. She didn't need a reason - chaos was in her blood.

Oh, how quickly he had lost track of the folk and their ways. He had almost forgotten the root of his own careless treachery.

But there was no time now to reminiscence.

He glanced at the window but saw only his reflection against the darkness outside.

This mansion was the same as the one in the real world, except that here each day was exactly the same - a loop of repeating time that ended each night with a midnight ball in this very room.

The king of this mansion could not leave its walls.

And now that duty fell to him.

He glanced at the throne in the corner of the conservatory, where they would expect him to sit and overlook their endless revels.

The room was already beginning to fill. A group of musicians in rust-colored uniforms squabbled over their instruments until they saw him and went quiet.

The rustling hush of ballgowns in motion poured in from all three doors.

"Your majesty, allow me to accompany you to your throne," Golda purred.

He nodded his head in assent and followed her without meaning to.

He even stood on the dais.

In twos and threes, the denizens of the mansion, who fancied themselves his subjects, went quiet as they entered and saw him.

The magnificent clock in the foyer struck once.

They all scurried off, as if getting into place for their nightly dance.

"No," he said.

They all froze, looking back at him.

The clock struck again.

He still surged with raw power from the battle with his brothers. He would never have a chance to resist once he let that magic fade. Nothing in this palace of apathy could ever feed his hunger like the pain he'd caused his brother's mortal queen.

Miranda...

Of course she was more than just his brother's consort. She had been Cullen's own loyal servant for years before turning on him. And now she knew the price of her betrayal.

He pushed the thoughts aside and steeled himself for the task at hand.

"I will not be your King of Midnight," he told the gathered crowd. "There will be no ball."

"What?" an older lady in an emerald gown asked. "What did he say?"

"He says there won't be a midnight ball," her partner whispered back loudly as the clock struck a third time.

"Why not?" the woman whined "He wouldn't be this way if that Jessica was still here."

"What did you say?" Cullen asked, allowing the glint of danger into his voice.

The clock sounded again.

"N-nothing," the woman answered, her lavender eyes widening.

"Did you say *if Jessica were still here*?" he asked, his voice cutting through the fog of ballgowns, cutting her with icy cold.

The clock sounded again as the woman shivered miserably and nodded.

"Where is she?" Cullen demanded.

"I-I," the woman stammered.

The clock sounded for the sixth time.

Cullen leapt from the dais and strode through the stunned crowd.

"Where is my Jessica?" he asked her.

The clock struck again and the woman cringed.

"Speak, mongrel," Cullen spat, his patience at its end.

But the woman was paralyzed with terror.

"Are you a woman or a statue?" His voice was light, teasing. But as he spoke he reached for her with his mind.

She glanced down at her feet, now rooted into the floor as solid stone.

He watched as the stone traveled up her body, overtaking her knees.

The clock struck again.

He had to get out soon.

"Th-the Queen of Silence took her," the woman managed as she watched her legs turn to granite.

"Took her where?" Cullen asked calmly.

The clock struck for the ninth time.

"T-to the countryside," the woman stammered. "Please, your majesty."

"I don't have all day," Cullen said briskly. "And you have considerably less than that. Where in the countryside?"

The stone inched up her torso.

"The north, your majesty," the woman's partner told him hurriedly. "She didn't say where, only that she would bring her to a cottage in the north."

The clock struck for the tenth time.

But Cullen knew where she was, at least roughly. It would have to be enough.

He flicked his wrist, ceasing the spell just as the woman's chin turned to stone.

She tipped into her partner's arms, and he nearly toppled under the weight of her.

"Please, your majesty," the man wailed. "Please turn her back."

The spell would wear off in a few hours, but for now their pain was feeding him, replenishing the energy he'd used for the spell, giving him what he needed to make it out.

The clock struck for the eleventh time.

Cullen turned back to the throne.

"So, are we going to dance?" Golda asked flirtatiously, following him.

He could see the fear in her eyes and it fed him, adding to his fuel until he felt almost sick with the excess.

"Do whatever you want," he murmured to her, moving faster now.

As the clock struck twelve he grabbed the throne in both fists and heaved it with all his might, expelling all the magic he had collected with a crash like thunder.

For a horrible heartbeat he was afraid he was wrong, that he had carried none of his heightened powers across the veil.

Then the throne exploded through the back wall, revealing a moonlit patch of garden and the darkness of the forest beyond.

Cullen launched himself through the hole in the wall before it could close up behind him.

"Your majesty," Golda's voice was plaintive.

He turned back and eyed the ball guests derisively.

"Wh-what should we do?" she asked.

"Whatever the hell you want," he said, turning away from his would be subjects.

He placed two fingers in his mouth and let out a loud, low whistle.

At first, only silence greeted him.

He felt the rumble of the ground even before he saw the pale shape of his ethereal stallion galloping toward him, glowing in the moonlight.

Nyx was all muscle under his snow-white velvet coat. The long, silken hair on his mane, tail and fetlocks floated backward as he moved, almost as if he were underwater, exaggerating the effect of his already frightening speed.

"Nyx," Cullen said as the beast thrust its massive forehead against his chest in greeting.

He stoked the pale cheek once, as the stallion snorted and pranced.

"Let's go," Cullen said, swinging onto his broad back.

The steed knew instinctively which way Cullen wanted him to go. He ran swiftly, hooves striking the loamy earth in a hellish cadence.

Cullen felt his body rhythm adjust to Nyx's stride until they were moving as one, as they always had.

As the moonlit landscape blurred past them, Cullen closed his eyes and tested the night air for the scent of tea roses.

3

JESSICA

Jessica Bell stepped out of her cottage and sucked in a deep breath of dewy morning air.

Aerin, her palomino pony, nickered and trotted over to greet her.

"Hello, my friend," Jessica said fondly, stroking the pony's creamy white mane.

She luxuriated in the smell from the fresh flowers all around, and the warmth from the sun kissing her cheeks and the velvet fur under her hand - all the pleasures of daily life.

But something was different today.

She shook her head to rid herself of the strange thought.

Every day was the same here - a perfect, sheltered life full of delicious meals and bright colors and every comfort Jessica could desire.

The silent queen had taken Jessica from that awful ballroom with the snickering dancers and deposited her here in the country, where she could enjoy a simple life of nature and study.

The queen had given her the pony, the house, and the time and freedom to read and relax as much as she liked.

Jessica knew she was being treated like a spoiled pet, but it was hard to mind when her life was so enjoyable.

Except that something was missing.

She just couldn't remember what.

Usually she had this feeling only in dreams. That was the only unpleasant part of her existence here. Nearly every night she had dreams where she searched frantically for something important, but never found it.

"Never mind," she said to herself. "Time for breakfast."

She and the pony took a leisurely stroll around the cottage to the grove in back, where a table waited under the weeping willow.

Each morning, a meal of fruit and tea appeared here.

She was relieved to see that today was no exception. The table had been covered with a lace cloth. A platter of sliced fruit glistened beside a cup and a steaming teapot.

"See, Aerin," she said. "It was nonsense."

The pony whiskered at the mention of her name and Jessica laughed.

She sat and took a bite of the fruit.

Normally, the flavor hit her like a waterfall, filling her senses with sweet, tart goodness.

Today it tasted more like the the fruit she remembered from her days in the other world - sweet and wholesome, but not a revelation.

She poured tea into the cup and watched the steam rise in a delicate mist.

She added fresh milk and reached for the sugar.

But when she turned back to her cup she could see the milk curdling on its surface.

The rancid chunks roiled in malevolent patterns, and

she swore she saw battles fought and storm clouds gathering in the swirls.

She stood abruptly.

Aerin snorted and spooked a little.

"Oh, I'm sorry, girl," Jessica crooned, feeling guilty. "It's just a strange day."

The pony minced back to her through the dewy grass.

"Shall we go pick flowers?" Jessica asked her.

The pony flicked her ears as if she understood.

And since their days were always the same, she probably did. Though she was used to watching her mistress eat breakfast with gusto first.

Aerin held angelically still as Jessica stepped onto a picturesque stump to mount her.

The pony trotted into the meadow and Jessica began to feel better as the air lifted her hair and the rhythm of the pony's steps lulled her into her usual frame of mind.

A gorgeous field of wild flowers grew just a short ride from her home. Jessica picked a bunch each day to bring back to the cottage with her, since the brass vase in the library was always empty each morning, no matter how many times she filled it with blooms. The scent of the wildflowers was so lovely in that peaceful space. The walls were lined with books of fairy lore and history, Jessica's favorite subject. It was impossible to be anything but happy there.

Generally, she spent most of her late morning studying and then began the routine again in the afternoon - a light meal, a ride and a study session in the library with the afternoon light teasing the pages until they blushed pink in the dying light.

Aerin carried her on cheerfully as she thought about the peacefulness of it all.

They arrived at the wild flower meadow just as the morning sunlight went warm and yellow.

Jessica dismounted and walked through the stems, admiring the brilliant blossoms. She selected a flower here and there as she walked, enjoying her stroll and feeling no need to hurry.

Aerin busied herself grazing on the lush grass and sweet clover.

A clump of buttercups, banana-yellow and perfect caught Jessica's eye. She bent to pick them, but felt a sharp, sweet pain on her hand.

She gasped and pulled her hand back.

"A bee sting," she realized out loud, gazing down at the small red dot between her thumb and forefinger.

That had certainly never happened before.

She put her hand to her mouth and looked around. Things looked the same as always.

Except for the sky.

Dark storm clouds had gathered over the hills that bordered the meadow, and they were moving in her direction. A grey shadowed darkened the land beneath them as they traveled.

"Aerin," she called out.

But the little mare was spooked. She cantered away, leaving Jessica alone to face the storm.

4

———

JESSICA

Jessica watched her pony flee.

She could see her cottage, but there was no way she would reach it on foot before the storm was on her.

As the clouds rolled in, she noticed something else headed her way - a figure on horseback, his dark hair whipping behind him with the speed of his approach. He seemed to be outpacing the storm itself.

Her heart stretched taut at the sight, as if it were reaching across the meadow for him.

She knew she should seek cover form the storm, but she found herself spellbound as the earth shivered with each hoofbeat of his massive steed. She could only stand there, stone-still, waiting for him as if she had grown roots.

The familiar stranger drew closer and closer, his snow white horse thundering relentlessly toward her.

"*Jessica,*" he called out as he reached her, his voice rough and raw.

How does he know my name?

The horse stopped a barely a stride from her, and the

man gazed feverishly down at her for a moment before leaping off and landing right in front of her.

She lifted her chin to meet his gaze.

He was huge, wildly masculine, yet something about his tragic expression told her she had nothing to fear from him.

"Jessica," he said again, reaching for her hand.

When he touched her skin, a surge of emotion overcame her, like something bubbling up from somewhere deep inside.

She closed her eyes and a long-forgotten memory surfaced.

She sits on a picnic blanket, her beloved journal in her hands, taking notes and trying not to be distracted by the giddy proximity of the god-like man who reclines beside her under the willow tree.

She is in love with him already.

But he is a wealthy man from the city, only visiting her small town for a short time.

Talking with her amuses him, but he will not return her love.

She knows this, and she doesn't mind. Loving him is enough for her, even if she has to keep it a secret.

"What are you writing about?"

His deep voice is slow and lazy, teasing her senses.

"Just notes for my book," she replies, feeling happiness rise in her like soda bubbles.

"Jessica," he says her name like a prayer as he sits up.

Now his size is more apparent. He dwarfs her, though she is not a small woman.

"Give me your hand," he murmurs in that deep, rough voice.

She acquiesces without a thought, lifting her hand and placing it against his, palm to palm.

"One day you will be my queen," he tells her.

It is a strange choice of words, but something inside her unlocks and she is overcome with wonder.

Before her eyes, delicate inky black vines grow around her ring finger and his, binding them together like magic.

"Jessica," he says again, bending to press his lips to hers for the first time.

His kiss fills her senses and she forgets the magic she has just seen. The pleasure of his mouth on hers is the only thing left in her world.

He pulls back.

"I love you," he tells her.

Universes seem to form and disintegrate in his eyes.

She is drowning in love, so happy that she can't even speak to tell him she feels the same.

JESSICA OPENED HER EYES.

Vines were growing over their fingers again now, the magic as wondrous now as it was the first time.

"Our rings," she breathed.

"I thought I'd lost you forever when mine disappeared," he murmured. "But it was only a temporary separation."

"We're together again," she whispered.

"Why did you leave me?" he asked.

She reached back to the memory, but nothing followed it.

"I don't know," she admitted. "I was in a ballroom and I hated it. The queen came and took me away, and I've been living in that little cottage."

She pointed at her cottage just downhill from the meadow.

The storm wind whipped through his hair as he gazed down at her pretty little home, unimpressed.

"I didn't have any memories before that," she told him. "Until now."

He clenched his jaw and she could sense his fury.

"So she trapped you here in the countryside," he growled, "and took your memories away?"

"No," she said. "She was so kind. I was unhappy in the ballroom, but now I have everything I could ever want."

"Can you leave?" he asked.

"I-I've never tried," she admitted. "I've never wanted to."

"How long have you been here?" he asked.

The words echoed strangely in her head.

How long *had* she been here?

She glanced back over the meadow. Her unchanging days here melted together, making it impossible to judge the passage of time.

"The seasons haven't changed," she thought out loud. "So it can't have been more than a few weeks. But it feels like maybe it's been longer than that."

He closed his eyes, looking troubled.

"How long has it been?" she asked, trying to understand what was upsetting him.

He looked the same as he had in her memory. His hair was dark and his face unlined. It couldn't have been that long.

Thunder rumbled close by, rumbling to her bones.

"Let's get out of here," he told her. "We can talk while we ride."

She allowed him to help her up onto the pale stallion.

The big horse pranced and snorted, but calmed when he leapt on after her.

She closed her eyes as he wrapped his arms around her,

soaking in his heat and the shivers of awareness his touch awoke.

He urged the horse on and the wildflowers began to blur past them.

They headed for the hills, leaving the little cottage far behind as a cold rain began to pound down. Jessica realized that she hadn't seen rain since she had arrived in the valley.

The cold drops felt like kisses on her cheeks, contrasting deliciously with the warm arms of the man who held her tight to his hard body as they thundered away from the only life she fully remembered.

***

Thanks for reading this sample of King of Pain!

Are you dying to find out what's going to happen when Jessica and Cullen try to escape the fae realm? Do you want to see what happens when Jessica starts to remember more details about the man she used to love? Are you ready for more magic, more adventure, and more steamy fae king goodness?

Then grab your copy now for the rest of the story:

https://www.tashablack.com/kingofpain.html

TASHA BLACK STARTER LIBRARY

Packed with steamy shifters, mischievous magic, billionaire superheroes, and plenty of HEAT, the Tasha Black Starter Library is the perfect way to dive into Tasha's unique brand of Romance with Bite!

Get your FREE books now at tashablack.com!

ABOUT THE AUTHOR

Tasha Black lives in a big old Victorian in a tiny college town. She loves reading anything she can get her hands on, writing sci fi & paranormal romance, and sipping pumpkin spice lattes.

Get all the latest info, and claim your FREE Tasha Black Starter Library at www.TashaBlack.com

Plus you'll get the chance for sneak peeks of upcoming titles and other cool stuff!

Keep in touch...
www.tashablack.com
authortashablack@gmail.com

facebook.com/romancewithbite
twitter.com/romancewithbite